Ruby's Present and Other Warm Tales of Christmas

Ruby's Present and Other Warm Tales of Christmas

Dan Salerno

Copyright © 2023 by Dan Salerno

All rights reserved.

ISBN: 979-8-9857725-4-8 (print)

ISBN: 979-8-9857725-5-5 (ebook)

No part of this book may be used or reproduced by any means, graphic, electronic, or mechanical, including photocopying, recording, taping or by any information storage retrieval system without the written permission of the copyright holder, except in the case of brief quotations embodied in critical articles and reviews.

This short story collection is a work of fiction. Any names, places, or events in this work of fiction are products of the author's imagination or are used fictitiously. Any resemblance to actual people, living or dead, events or places is coincidental and not intended by the writer.

Cover design by Roger Heldt

Back cover author photo by Deborah Salerno

ALSO BY DAN SALERNO

20 Short Ones: 20 Tales of Hope

Metropolis: Tales from a Small Town

A note about these stories

Dan had been working on these "warm tales of Christmas" at the time of his sudden death in June 2023. Except for a few editing corrections (spelling, grammar, punctuation), they appear here as we found them on his computer.

We hope you will read gently around any rough spots you may encounter and appreciate the message of love, tolerance, and social justice that resonates throughout these stories and characterized our brother's life. Special thanks to all friends, family, churches, and communities who helped bring this book to reality.

Dan was a man of faith. He was also a romantic and had a wicked sense of humor. We believe you will find these qualities in abundance in the stories that follow.

The Salerno Committee to Publish Dan's Book

November 1, 2023

Table of Contents

'Tis the Season // 1
A Brooklyn Christmas // 13
Abby // 23
Ashley's Wish // 35
At the Odeon // 47
Comfort and Joy // 57
Dillon // 69
Estabon // 81
Haley Goes to South Haven // 93
Icing on the Cake // 103
Jersey and the KIA // 121
Jon and Keisha at St. Bart's // 133
Kristie's Red Potato Skillet // 147
Lunch Lady // 161
Missy Gets Dancing Lessons // 173
Ruby's Present // 183
Saree to the Rescue // 193
The Emergency Room // 205
The Redemption of Campbell // 219
Winnie's Socks // 231

ABOUT THE AUTHOR // 243

'Tis the Season

Betty was working the circulation desk at the main branch of the Kalamazoo Public Library. It was December 22nd and snowing good and hard outside. On her lunch break she walked a few blocks down Rose Street to Just Good Food to grab a chicken curry salad on rye.

She had grown up in Milwood but lived in Cooper's Landing apartments off G Avenue in a two-bedroom she shared with Monica, her best friend from high school. For two years, while earning her Master's degree in Library Science, she had her own place in the student ghetto on Wheaton Street. But as she began to settle into her mid-twenties, living within hearing distance of out-of-control co-ed parties had lost its appeal.

Her mother had named her after Betty Hutton, which would have been fine if it had been 1958. On the other hand, for as long as she could remember, she had been the only Betty. Going to St. Monica's grade school, her teachers had tried extra hard not to single her out for any reason, not that Betty gave them cause. She wasn't outwardly rebellious, but beneath the surface, where it counted, she was an intellectual adventurist.

Her grandparents had been of the '60s generation that had the annoying habit of questioning everything. Which led to her own parents questioning nothing, being very content to go with the flow. Which was sort of ironic because they had birthed a daughter who had grown into a 5'2" tall bastion of progressive thinking.

As a matter of fact, the first periodical that Betty subscribed to as a nine-year-old was *The Catholic Worker* newspaper, the mouthpiece of a social justice movement that was continually second-guessing the federal government and any other bureaucracy that seemed too big for its britches.

She sat eating her sandwich, reading the latest issue of the *Worker*. Her favorite columns were the ones that spoke to the goings-on around the Catholic Worker Farm in upstate New York – which grew produce for meals at Joseph House and Maryhouse, and a column focused on assorted guests who visited Joseph House and Maryhouse – which together served as the national headquarters of the movement in New York City that combined serving the poor with living with them in voluntary poverty.

In the olden days, Joseph House used to have a guest book placed near the front entrance, next to the large kitchen. The book was used to record the musings of visitors, staff, and homeless folks who had come off the street to share their lives.

The whole idea, according to Peter Maurin, who with Dorothy Day, founded the movement in the depths of the Great Depression, was to 'build a new society within the shell of the old,' where it was easier to do good through daily acts of mercy while living in community.

While reading the newspaper, Betty had imagined what Mary House felt like, where formerly homeless women came to live. It was one thing to describe the trials and challenges of living together in simplicity. It was quite another to be there on the ground level. Did Maryhouse have a lot of hallways and other nooks and crannies, out of the main flow of traffic? Areas where a person could get away and recoup for a few minutes before getting on with their day? Or was it more like a college dorm, where, instead of students making racket and engaging in conversation till the wee hours, it was a continual flow of emergency-type situations? She guessed that it was somewhere in-between.

She felt that the live-in volunteers who so openly described their lives in the newspaper were nothing short of heroic. Betty knew she didn't have the temperament to stay calm in the middle of dealing with so many people's unique life situations.

Yet she always offered a smile when library patrons came to her, frustrated with not being able to find the book they were looking for. Searching for fiction in the non-fiction section, not knowing that the books were arranged in alphabetical order, by author. Or not having a clue where the computers were located that you could use to access the Foundation Center's software.

As Betty was about to turn the page of the newspaper, a voice interrupted her thoughts.

"Excuse me." The tone was hospitable, approachable, and she perceived a bit of humor to it. The thing was, at that moment, she wasn't eager to extend herself over the lunch hour if she didn't have to leave her inner oasis.

She turned to look at the man who had spoken to her. He was just as short as she was. But she detected something in his eyes. They were green and exuded empathy like an evocative cologne. Just a dab was good for the whole day. Only what he had was coming from deep inside him.

Betty couldn't help but respond. "Can I help you?"

If he were as empathetic as he looked, couldn't he sense that she could use this noontime respite from the workplace?

For his part, Ruel was 37 years old, having gotten a postgraduate degree in social research at Hunter College, which was part of the City University of New York. It was a degree that usually resulted in work for advertising companies, public relations firms, or research tanks, after you'd had a few years to establish your experience. But he wasn't a native New Yorker, so shortly after graduation, he moved back to Kalamazoo.

For 12 years, he had worked for Bronson Hospital's marketing department. Then he had recently switched gears, got lucky, and was hired by the Kalamazoo Valley Museum to develop promotional materials and educational modules.

"I was wondering if you wouldn't mind telling me what you're eating. It looks delicious."

Betty put down her newspaper before answering. "It's chicken curry salad."

"Is it as good as it looks?"

"Well, I've been told they sell tons of it a week, so lots of people must enjoy it."

"I usually stick with creamy potato and broccoli soup, but I'm pretty sure there isn't a boiling 50-gallon caldron of it in the basement."

She laughed. *This guy is funny. And good-looking*, she thought. *That's two out of three!*

She stuck out her hand. "I'm Betty Boylston."

He shook it. "Ruel Stavinsky."

She motioned for him to join her.

Almost as soon as Ruel sat down, she began to feel increasingly comfortable.

After six years at the library, she had advanced herself to assistant librarian, in charge of elementary education programming. She spent a good chunk of time with the Communities In Schools program, thinking up creative ways to promote literacy.

"This is a really funky place, isn't it?" Ruel was referring to Just Good Food's basement location, with old photos on the wall. And a menu board that was a series of poetic descriptions of each sandwich offered, set up in a row across the deli counter.

"Yeah, it is. I love it. It's my favorite downtown place to eat."

"I've only been here a couple of times."

"So, the sandwich sign outside snagged your interest?"

"That, and the fact that I work right across the street."

"You work for Central City Parking?" (the guardian of Kalamazoo's parking meters).

"No. The Museum."

Ironically, the Kalamazoo Valley Museum was another of Betty's favorite places. She regularly went there to take in the new exhibits. She always walked up the stairs to the second floor slowly, viewing the displays of local memorabilia that stretched from the bottom floor to the third, like a giant shadow box. The juxtaposition of historic periods and pieces was a reminder of time's inevitable move forward.

"What a great place to work!"

"Well, so far, it's been great. How about yourself?"

Betty folded up her newspaper before answering. "I'm a librarian at the Public Library, down the street."

He laughed.

"I didn't realize that being a librarian was such a funny job."

"I'm sorry, it's just that whenever someone mentions that word, I think back to my youngest sister's college graduation. There were something like 25 students who received their Master's degree in Library Science that Spring. All sitting together, when their dean congratulated them, the whole group turned to the audience, put their pointer fingers to their lips, and whispered, 'Shhh!' It was great."

She smiled. "We tend to be a fun crowd."

"What's your favorite book?"

"That would be Proverbs, from the Bible."

Actually, it was a section from the first chapter of Proverbs that had become her favorite. She softly spoke:

Wisdom shouts in the streets.
She cries in the public square.
She calls to the crowds along the main street,
to those gathered in front of the city gate:
'How long, you simpletons,
will you insist on being simpleminded?
How long will you mockers relish your mocking?
How long will you fools hate knowledge?
Come and listen to my counsel.
I'll share my heart with you
and make you wise.'

Ruel nodded his head. "I love the personification of wisdom."

"What if it's not a personification?"

"What do you mean?"

"Wisdom could be seen as a living, breathing thing."

"No kidding?"

Betty nodded her head.

After eight years at St. Monica's, Betty had transferred to Loy Norrix High School, where she became involved in the Drama Department. She had been instantly smitten. The enchanting atmosphere of the theatre, especially after she discovered the backstage area. She knew that she wasn't an actress. What really interested her was what took place behind the scenes. It was a separate world from anything she had ever experienced. It was the closest thing to make-believe that she had come across, and it was nothing short of hypnotic.

During her senior year, Miss MacMurphy had elected to put on a production of "The Diary of Anne Frank," which naturally lent itself to philosophical-minded discussions about the existence of good and evil.

At the cast party after closing night, Betty sat next to Benjamin Goldberg, who was the proud owner of a headful of jet-black curly hair. His eyes were dark and piercing, which made him look like a young Bob Dylan. All during the practice and run of the play, Betty had admired Benjamin from afar as he played the part of Peter Van Daan. So, when she saw him sitting down, absent-mindedly munching some tortilla chips, in-between conversations, she snapped up the chance to engage him in chit-chat. To her surprise, she found they had a lot in common. But they never had the opportunity to follow up on the conversation. (You know how it tends to go in high school. So much depends upon sheer luck and moxie.)

It was this very frustrating experience that had caused her to vow never to waste time engaging in romantic nonsense. She stuck to the non-fiction section after that.

Nonetheless, she found herself giving Ruel a good look-over before reciting another section of Proverbs (3:19) from memory:

By wisdom the Lord founded the earth,
by understanding he created the heavens.
By his knowledge the deep fountains of the earth
burst forth, and the dew settles beneath the night sky.

"So, you're quite the evangelical, aren't you?"
"Not really."
"But you seem to know a lot of scripture."
She laughed. "I'm attracted to the poetic imagery of it."
"You aren't religious?"
"No, but I absolutely love God."
"Then this must be one of your favorite times of year."

Ruel's own frame of reference was mostly a Jewish one. Hanukah and the menorah, especially the shamash candle, had fascinated him. He loved that there was a candle set aside for purely practical reasons.

"Well, if you mean celebrating the birth of Jesus, it is. But..."

She paused before continuing. The whole subject of Christmas was a sore spot. When Christmas came around it only accentuated the fact that Betty had no real spiritual soulmate. And that hurt deeply.

"But?"

She smiled before continuing. It was warm, genuine, inviting, and one of her best features. "But why do we, as humans, have a tendency to take such beautifully simple spiritual truths and complicate them?"

Ruel smiled. "Isn't there a saying about that?"

"Pardon?"

"'Perfect love casts out fear?' It's in the Bible, right?"

"Maybe John was being ironic."

Ruel shook his head. "He set up that scripture by talking about how God is love, and living in love makes us one with God."

"How would you know that? I mean, no offense or anything. Is that in the Torah?"

Ruel nodded. "There's plenty about love in the Torah."

"For instance?"

"For instance, Abraham loving God so much that he was willing to sacrifice his son Isaac."

"But that's trust, not love."

Ruel smiled. "But it's a start, isn't it?"

Betty thought about her own job. She trusted the staff who re-stacked the library shelves to put books back in their proper places. She trusted the associates working the circulation desk to give the right information to help customers find the books they were looking for. She trusted every person who used the checkout kiosks to return the books on time. Then it dawned on her, almost like a revelation: Without trust, a library wouldn't be possible.

She blurted out: "So, could a lack of trust be ruining my experience of Christmas?"

Ruel edged a bit closer. "I can't answer that for you. But usually belief follows faith."

"Meaning you have to trust in order to believe."

"Right."

"Well, that sort of sucks."

Ruel unsuccessfully tried to stifle a laugh.

"If we need to believe in something to have faith, then that's quite a stumbling block to begin with." Betty was looking straight at Ruel. "Not to mention the fact that the playing field is woefully skewed in favor of naivety."

"Naivety isn't the same thing as faith."

Betty took a last bite of her sandwich before continuing. "Christmastime only seems to highlight what we're talking about."

As soon as the words came out of her mouth, Betty realized that she was in a tug of war with her emotions. She was enjoying the conversation with Ruel, and she found him to be a very interesting guy. But there was another part of her that was sending out warning signals, triggered by missteps from her past. Like the lack of follow-up with Benjamin, the curly-haired thespian from high school.

"Why bother to set myself up for another letdown?" she thought. "I'm not hanging out with Ruel in the student union, and I'm not in my 20s anymore."

"Everybody gets hurt at some point," he said, almost as if he were reading Betty's mind. "But when someone steps on your toes, are you going to get up and keep dancing or get off the dance floor?"

"Especially at Christmastime, right?"

"How so?" Ruel asked.

"This time of year, there are tons more folks out on the dance floor, and unless you're a smooth dancer to begin with, the chances of getting stepped on are a lot higher."

Ruel laughed at the image of a room full of people tripping the light fantastic to the tune of "I'm Dreaming of a White Christmas."

Which was ironic, because right then, Betty's mind chose to take her back to the movie within which that very song was sung. "Why aren't there good crooners like Bing Crosby anymore?" she thought. "And didn't he look charming all dressed up in a cardigan, smoking a pipe, and stealing a sandwich in the middle of the night when a very young and beautiful Rosemary Clooney just happens to show up?"

Ruel caught the far-away look in her eyes. "You're daydreaming, aren't you?"

She recovered nicely. "No, I just got sidetracked a bit at your dancing floor reference."

"Does it boil down to once bitten, twice shy?"

"I may be a progressive, but I'm also practical when it comes to matters of the heart."

As the words came out of her mouth, she winced.

For his part, Ruel slowly reached into his coat pocket and retrieved a piece of paper that had his grocery list on it. He tore off a small piece and began to write.

Betty's curiosity got the better of her, and she glanced at the list. "You want me to do part of your grocery shopping?"

He ignored the comment and looked straight into her eyes as he gently placed the piece of paper in her hand.

"Here's my phone number. You know my name and where I work."

She took the paper and put it in her purse. Summoning up all the courage she had in her, she kept the conversation going. "I'll do you one better. Give me your cell phone."

Ruel obediently handed it over.

Betty took it and punched in her number. "You've got mine now as well."

He smiled as he got up to go back to work. "Thank you."

"For what?"

"For trusting me."

She smiled back. "'Tis the season!"

Dan Salerno

A Brooklyn Christmas

Mickey was driving up Myrtle Avenue, headed to the Glendale Diner. He was on staff at a children's ministry focused on inner-city kids in the boroughs of New York City. He lived in the Bushwick neighborhood of Brooklyn, on Central Avenue, in an apartment (above a pizzeria) that he shared with two other ministry team members. The apartment building was located one very long block down the street from the church.

Everyone on the team worked six days, and 50-plus-hour weeks were the norm. So, on his day off, Mickey was looking forward to some peace and quiet. He chose the Glendale Diner because it had good food, and it was just far enough away, in Queens, from the ministry headquarters to have a sense of getting away from it all without having to go into Manhattan.

Mickey was really looking forward to having two poached eggs, two strips of crispy bacon, American fries, and whole wheat toast, dry with coffee. Normally he had cold cereal for breakfast, so eating out was a real treat. He had picked up a copy of the New York Times and had a smile on his face as he opened the door to the diner and sat down at a booth, out of the way of customer traffic. He usually got there around 9:30, when most of the early morning work-related rush was over.

After the waitress took his order, Mickey began to scan the Times front page. He became engrossed in the news until he heard a voice ask: "Mind if I join you?"

Having time to yourself as a member of a ministry team was a rare thing, and when the opportunity presented itself, you jumped on it. A whole day of free time was like a week on the beach in a condo. But Mickey didn't want to be rude, so he looked up. To his surprise, it was Allie DeFranco, another member of the team.

"Sure, have a seat," he answered.

It was a bit awkward for Mickey because he really didn't know Allie outside of work. Something like 97 percent of all 150 workers in the street ministry division were single, and about 75 percent were women. Although the teams were as integrated as possible, after the workday was complete, women usually hung out with women and guys hung out with guys.

Allie was naturally outgoing and had a smile that lit up her face. It was accentuated with an impossibly curly head of dark chestnut-brown hair. She had worked her way up in the ranks of the street division to head of curriculum. Which meant that Allie oversaw the department that created the "Sunday school" lessons taught by all 14 street divisions – each division being responsible for a neighborhood.

She was the epitome of a people person. In fact, she seemed to have a built-in radar that kept her from spending too much time alone. Mickey, on the other hand, treasured solitude. At the end of a long day spent with adults preparing for the day's outreach, and then with kids, and then with their families, he craved peace and quiet. Not so with Allie.

"So, how's it going?" she asked. The fact that she didn't know Mickey outside of work didn't bother her in the slightest. Allie had seen him when she walked into the diner and instantly walked up to his booth.

Mickey gave a smile before answering, "Good, and you?"

His mother had taught Mickey good manners. His father had died suddenly of a massive stroke when he was six, leaving his mom to look after three young children, with Mickey being the youngest. Her example had taught him how to be polite, no matter how you were feeling on the inside.

"I'm doing great!" she answered. "We've got the day off, next week's lesson plans are done, and it's only two weeks before Christmas!"

For ministry team members, that meant double duty on Saturdays at the ministry's headquarters. That's when all the teams stayed in Brooklyn to minister to local kids who were bussed in from every Brooklyn neighborhood.

Normally, there would be three services. But on the two Saturdays before Christmas, it was doubled. The idea was to get as many children as possible to come and receive a Christmas message, with presents and candy to take home. For many of the kids who came, this would be their only Christmas experience.

Allie really looked forward to the double duty. Her heart was focused on impacting the lives of as many kids as she could during this special season. Her own childhood had been one of growing up on a small farm in British Columbia. Her parents were very close, and the family of two girls were nurtured by the warmth of that closeness.

It was a blessing that she had this foundation of love from an early age because, when she was 10, her mother was killed in a traffic accident as she was on her way to Vancouver to visit her sister. All at once, Allie's world was sent spinning. Her father became withdrawn for a while, but he found comfort in the friendships that developed at the family's church. Allie too had held on to those friendships and her faith in the Eternal One, which helped soften the blow.

For Mickey's mother, on the other hand, her career as a cardiac nurse became her lifeline. She worked her way up to head nurse of the unit. She didn't have the luxury of grieving when her husband left the family when Mickey was 11. Survival became her coping mechanism, and although she had friends, the friendships weren't especially close. Mickey experienced firsthand, the effect of losing someone you loved. He was understandably reluctant to have that happen again.

"Christmas," Mickey repeated the word, mulling it over in his mind.

Allie intuitively sensed an emotional wound close to the surface. "Anything wrong?"

"It's nothing, really." That had been his standard answer when his mom had asked the same question growing up. He saw how hard she worked and how tired she was after the end of a 12-hour shift. If she could cope, so could he.

"I really didn't mean to pry." Allie's eyes exuded empathy, not leaving any chance to misinterpret the sincerity of her concern.

"I'm sorry," Mickey said, "I guess I'm not feeling the Christmas spirit yet."

As if on cue, the waitress came to take Allie's order, leaving a natural pause in the conversation to reconsider what would come next.

Allie smiled again and decided to take another path towards getting to know Mickey. "People are so interesting, don't you think? Especially kids!"

This brought a smile to Mickey's face. He truly enjoyed the time spent with the kids on the street. That's what he lived for. It was the adults that presented the biggest challenges. "Yeah, I'm always blown away by how resilient they are."

"It's like God knew we needed built-in shock absorbers for the human spirit."

Mickey paused a moment before answering. "I think the reason I enjoy the kids so much is that I realize that I'm just like them. I mean, emotionally, I can relate."

This was a first for him. He had never discussed this part of growing up with anyone.

"How so?"

"I mean, the kids we interact with, they all have so much to deal with. You and I have resources to help us, but they don't. They're emotional orphans."

"That's a good way of putting it," Allie agreed.

Then she told a story about when she was new to the ministry. One of the kids asked Allie to walk him home after the teaching time was over. He was a tough kid, and she was surprised that he would ask her to do that. He lived in a public housing project right across from the park where the team had set up. As Allie and the boy crossed the street, she noticed he looked worried.

She asked him what was going on, and he said he'd forgotten to tell his dad that he wasn't coming right home after school. Allie tried to ease his mind and told him not to worry about it, offering to explain the situation to his father. But he shook his head and said, "You don't know my dad."

Allie and the boy were a few steps away from the lobby of the public housing project when the boy reached up and pulled her hand.

"Here he comes," he said, pointing to a man walking towards them. His dad was holding something in his left hand, but Allie couldn't quite make out what it was. As he got closer, she saw it was a piece of a tree branch.

The boy's father made a motion as if to swing it towards his son, but at the last instant he threw the branch to the side, with a disgusted look on his face. "Boy," he said, completely ignoring Allie. "Don't you ever make me go looking for you again!" Then he turned to Allie. "He's lucky that he walked home with you today."

Allie stopped to take a breath.

"Wow," Mickey said.

"Yeah, wow."

Allie and Mickey both realized that the story she just told could be duplicated a hundred times over. Growing up poor in the inner city was never easy.

"So, what's your story?" she softly asked. Their food had arrived, but they were ignoring it.

"My dad," Mickey slowly began. "He left us when I was eleven."

"I'm sorry," Allie was in the moment, feeling his loss.

"That wasn't actually the hard part," he continued. "Seeing how it affected my mom, that was tough. She closed herself off. There were three sons she instantly became responsible for, and she was working full time just to put food on the table."

"Sounds like your mom was a very strong woman."

Mickey looked directly at Allie for the first time and saw the compassion in her brown eyes.

"Too strong. She was basically functioning as both parents and was really overwhelmed."

"She must have loved you tremendously."

"At the time, I didn't understand," Mickey said, "I figured if this is what losing someone you love is like, I don't want that to happen ever again."

After Allie's mom passed away, she had the benefit of a dad who understood the importance of emotionally relating to his daughters. He had demonstrated that love by teaching them to play baseball, by going to their soccer games, by laughing with them, and by staying up when they came home from dates so they could tell him the details.

"I lost my mom when I was your age," she said. "At first, my dad and my sister were all in a state of shock. But my dad, he didn't close down. His faith kept him going."

Mickey looked surprised. "It did?"

"Yes."

Funny that being in ministry didn't mean that all of life's challenges had somehow been resolved.

"How?" was all he could ask.

"Well, for one thing, Dad realized that he wasn't alone. He believed that God was with him and would help him through a difficult time."

"How did your mom die?"

"It was a freak traffic accident," Allie explained. "She was driving, on the way to visit my aunt. The driver of an oncoming car moved into her lane, and Mom didn't react in time. She was hit head-on. Overnight, Dad became a single parent."

Mickey swallowed hard, knowing he might be pushing the envelope to go on. "What was their relationship like? I mean, as far as you could see?"

"Dad and Mom absolutely adored each other," she answered without hesitation. "The happiest part of my dad's day was when he came home and hugged my mom. He couldn't wait to hold her. Then he'd turn to us and give us a bunch of sloppy kisses until we started laughing."

"That's great," Mickey said. He could appreciate the effect that the foundation of childhood love had on her.

"It was," she said. "But I realize that I've got an obligation to pass it on. That's why I came to the ministry in the first place, and it's what keeps me going. I know it can be a hassle sometimes, but I try not to let that get in the way of how I treat the kids. They always come first."

Mickey was curious. He also realized that neither one of them had touched their food, so he pointed to his plate. "You know what they say about breakfast, right?"

Allie smiled. "What? Did you use to work for Kellogg's?"

He smiled, full tilt. "I was only going to say that we should probably start eating before all this gets cold."

"How long have you been the spokesperson for the Breakfast Institute of America?" she asked, barely stifling a smile of her own.

This time, he laughed before speaking. "I'm only a part-time consultant." He took a good look at what she was eating. "Do you always order sunny side up?"

"Yep. You can tell a lot about a person just by having breakfast with them."

"Is that so?"

"Absolutely! If they order poached, they're probably on the conservative side. If they order scrambled, watch out, because they're free-falling and really aren't into details. And if they order oatmeal, run away."

"You're good."

"Years of practice. And we haven't even gotten into pop-tarts, cereal bars, or yogurt."

Mickey smiled again, realizing that Allie had gently positioned herself into his life. She was polite, engaging, and genuinely empathetic.

"Do you mind if I ask what you usually do on your day off?" he asked.

"After six days of structure, I love to be spontaneous in the morning and then leave time to hang out with some of the kids in the afternoon, after they're out of school."

He was impressed. This was going beyond any work requirement and spoke of true dedication. "That's amazing."

Allie quickly shook her head. "It's a lot of fun. I get to know the kids and the kids' parents a little better. Plus, I get to pick the ones who need a little TLC."

Allie had a good reason to be this proactive and involved. Right after her mom died, a grade school teacher had taken the time to ask Allie if everything was okay. She had noticed that Allie's participation in class had fallen off, and her grades. It was the teacher's ability to listen that helped Allie through a rocky part of her life. It was just as important to her as her father's faith.

It was going on 10:30. By this time, they had both finished eating their breakfast, yet Mickey didn't want the conversation to end.

"Would you like to hang out a bit more?" he asked, trying not to appear too hopeful.

For her part, Allie had enjoyed her interaction with Mickey. She was sociable but didn't have a lot of friends on the ministry team outside of the female persuasion. It was easy for her to chat with him, and the time they had already spent had flown by.

"Well," she smiled, "The rest of the day, until school is out, is free. How about going into the city and heading to Central Park?" Allie's ministry team was responsible for a few blocks of Spanish Harlem, and she could easily get to it from there.

"Sounds good," Mickey began, standing up and making a move to help Allie put on her coat. "I can drive us back to Bushwick, and we can take the J train from there."

Mickey wasn't the type to initiate relationships with women. Not that he was shy, but difficulties relating to his mom had transferred over to most females. The bottom line was that the sheer force of years of frustration had built up an emotional wall that got in the way of much interaction beyond superficial pleasantries. But with Allie, he found himself curiously open.

Being witty, smart, warm, and wholesomely pretty, Allie had no trouble attracting guys from the time she was a teenager. Most of them were not her intellectual equal, and those who were often proved to be emotionally out to lunch. Suffice to say that Allie had a wealth of dating experience, but mostly in group situations. Hence, she was used to having guy friends, but nothing seriously romantic.

"Oh, a gentleman in the ministry!" Allie teased as she held open her arms so Mickey could place her coat on her shoulders. She noticed how his hazel eyes were particularly deep.

She flipped her auburn hair over the coat's collar and buttoned it up. As they finished paying their bills, Mickey looked out the window of the diner, and a huge grin slowly came across his face. "Look at that. It's snowing!"

"I'm a huge fan of snow around Christmas time," she said as they walked out of the diner. "You should probably know that about me."

Abby

Winter was Abby's favorite season. She loved the snow. She loved the wind. She loved the way the stars appeared brighter in the sky. She loved everything about it. Even the branches on the trees, stripped bare. For Abby, it wasn't bleak; it was beautiful in all its austerity.

And because Christmas fell in the middle of it, she especially loved the season. She loved visiting her favorite Christmas tree lot and taking the time to choose just the right one for her living room. Big enough so that the smell of evergreen permeated the entire apartment, but small enough so that she could see out her living room window, which was decorated on the outside. So it was with great anticipation that the 42-year-old left the hospital where she worked as a critical care nurse. She headed to the Gull Road Market, which sold trees this time of year.

Getting out of her red Chevy Volt, she was greeted by Granger, the owner's son. Granger had been home for about a week, taking a break from his job on Wall Street to help his family.

"Merry Christmas!" she offered.

"Merry Christmas to you, too!"

"What sort of tree are you looking for? Scotch Pine? Spruce?"

Abby's eyes widened at the large selection spread out in front of her. "I'm more interested in the size than the type."

Granger smiled in acknowledgement. "The taller ones are in the back. Smaller ones are up front, and every other size is in-between."

"How about heading for a middle section then?"

"Sounds good."

They walked in silence for a few minutes until Abby was smitten with a gorgeous Scotch pine that was bursting with needles, looking radiant in its fullness.

Abby pointed to it. "This one's great! It's absolutely perfect."

"There's something to be said for getting your tree ahead of the crowd."

She beamed at the remark. Ever since she was a little girl, Abby had been one step ahead of everyone else. In fact, she was born prematurely, about two weeks before her due date, which didn't really bother her mother, Suzette. Mainly because Suzette was the same way. Like mother, like daughter.

At any rate, from those first months of her life, Abby had shown a remarkable ability to figure things out quicker than her peers. She was always in the top percentile in infant development, be it crawling, walking, talking, eating by herself, being potty-trained, cutting her first teeth, and subsequently losing them for permanent.

Once she started kindergarten, Abby impressed her teacher by requesting additional books in the classroom library after having read through them all in less than two months' time. Actually, there wasn't a practical reason why she asked her teacher's assistance because Abby had marched herself to the public library when she was five to get a card. She even had the foresight to bring ID with her.

"I don't know why I'm so good at life's logistics, except for relationships," she was thinking when her thought process was interrupted by a gentle tap from Granger.

"Excuse me, but do you need a stand with the tree?"

"No, thanks. I've got one."

"There's nothing like the smell of evergreen to get you in the mood for Christmas, is there?" he asked.

Granger was wondering why Abby was so determined-looking. All sorts of folks came to his lot, but they normally weren't rushed, at least not this early in the season. But Abby gave the impression that she was on a mission from the second she stepped out of her car.

"Oh, I love how the scent really fills up the apartment!" She answered, pausing a second to take a good look at Granger. "I don't believe I've met you before," she added.

Since Abby had been going to the Gull Road Market for a number of years, she had come to know Jerry Holstead and his wife, Molly. They were a sweet couple whose three children had long since moved away from home. While Abby knew they had a son, she had never met him.

"I'm Granger," he said, offering a handshake and a smile by way of an introduction. "Jerry and Molly are my parents."

"Do you live around here?" Abby couldn't help but ask the question, mostly out of an unrelenting curiosity that had nothing to do with romance. Although it didn't hurt that Granger was exactly six feet tall, remarkably in shape for a 45-year-old, with a thick head of premature gray hair and a salt-and-pepper beard.

Granger laughed. "I grew up here, but sad to say, I've lived most of my adult life in Manhattan."

"Why would that make you sad?"

"Because if Wall Street were here, I'd be a happy man."

"Really?" Now he had Abby genuinely intrigued. Why would someone remain in New York when they didn't need to be there? What was holding him back?

"I manage a mutual fund. My apartment is an eight-minute walk from work, and everything I need is only a few blocks away."

Abby looked into Granger's eyes and could see that all the convenience of the Big Apple still left something lacking.

"Normally you don't come home for the holidays, do you?" It wasn't exactly detective work on her part to notice this; after all, she'd been coming to Gull Road Market for over eight years and had never run into him.

"I sort of had a Christmas tradition of working up to Christmas Eve and then heading for Colorado," he answered.

For the past 12 years, that place had been Aspen. Part of his tradition was to book a ski lodge with his girlfriend, Becky, who was an attorney at a firm serving higher-end clients. They both earned great salaries with careers that didn't include anything of substance outside of the office.

"Do you have a family tradition to celebrate the season?" he asked.

Abby's eyes narrowed slightly as she bit her lip. She didn't want to tell Granger that this would be a Christmas with no boyfriend, prospects, or otherwise. How could she explain the long string of significant-other-less holidays? Sure, she had friends. Plenty of them came from the hospital – including surgeons, cardiologists, respiratory therapists, radiologists, and a host of nurses. Plenty of guy pals but no boyfriend.

Case in point was her latest relationship fiasco, Dr. Austin Mellish. After six months, he had yet to pick up the tab for dinner. That is, when he was free to have one. Normally, it had been a sandwich hastily eaten in the hospital cafeteria with promises to do something 'romantic' later. Abby wasn't exactly torn apart when he had finally called with a dinner invitation, texting to cancel it at the last minute. She called him back, canceling their friendship.

Before the good doctor, it had been Reilly. He was a pure-bred Irishman from Galway who had earned his medical degree from the University of Michigan. He had gone out with Abby while completing his internship at the hospital where she worked. Reilly was an attractive guy with thick, wavy black hair and an easy smile to go along with his Celtic wit. He had excellent bedside manner with his patients, but unfortunately, that was where his focus stopped. He had no sense of the need for a deep relationship. He had been oblivious to Abby's thirst for emotional intimacy.

And it wasn't just doctors who were guilty of relational negligence. For Abby, there seemed to be a real lack of ability for the middle-aged men in her life to engage in meaningful conversation beyond sports scores, retirement plans, and fantasy football.

"What is it with these guys?" she thought. "Is it them, or is something seriously wrong with me to keep attracting such people's interest?"

The very idea of that had been enough to send her into the kitchen for a glass of wine.

Back at Gull Road Market, Abby summoned up the nerve to give Granger a straight answer. "I plan to spend Christmas Eve with my parents in town and then Christmas with my sister and her family."

"That's who you're spending the holiday with, but what about tradition? What does your family do to celebrate?"

Granger knew he was pushing it by asking Abby to go a bit deeper, but he figured, "What the heck? I haven't been home for Christmas for years, so why not take a chance?"

And besides, for some reason, which he was trying to figure out, he was finding himself attracted to her.

"We eat, a lot. All of us are good cooks. So, we always wind up spending time in the kitchen. The interesting thing is that we aren't at all like the 'too many cooks spoil the soup' type of people."

Some of Abby's best childhood memories involved spending time with her mom over the stove. It began with learning how to bake bread when she was a teenager, branching out to experiment with different types of flour. Sharing laughter with her mother while kneading dough had been a natural preventative to the typical drifting apart that happens between parents and children in those teenage years. The camaraderie strengthened an emotional intimacy that remained strong throughout Abby's life.

Ironically, it was because of these childhood memories that Abby experienced an odd sort of loneliness when preparing meals at home by herself. She yearned for someone to share those types of intimate moments.

"Once you invite me over, I can count on some home cooking?" Granger laughed a little self-consciously, trying to keep the conversation light. He had no idea of the weight of the subject matter on Abby's heart.

"Actually, I haven't been doing much from scratch lately," Abby confessed, feeling the blood rushing to her cheeks.

Granger lifted his eyebrows a bit, sending a gentle invitation to continue the thought.

"I mean, when I was a kid, I loved spending time with mom in the kitchen. And every holiday when my family gets together, it's the same sort of thing. Which makes me miss it during the in-between times. You know what they say: 'If you can't stand the heat...'"

"...steer away from the places that remind you of what you miss."

"That's why you didn't head to Colorado this Christmas?"

He nodded his head before answering. "Nothing against Colorado, but the skiing isn't quite as good solo, especially during the holidays."

"Sort of hard to sit by the yuletide fire in the lodge curling up with a good book when everyone else is cuddling up with someone?"

"Truer words were never spoken."

There was a pause in the conversation as Granger helped Abby tie her Christmas tree to the top of her car. He was very careful to be sure it was snug. It was funny how, after all those years away from the family's tree farm, he still remembered the tricks of the trade. He made a secure slipknot to finish off his work, allowing for a little leeway to keep the needle loss to a minimum.

He was also struck by how much his spirit of adventure was still there, even after having been recently burned in the relationship department. The timing of Becky's pre-holiday departure was awful, but as soon as the initial shock of it wore off, Granger had been the first to admit that their friendship was going nowhere. He had driven himself from New York to Michigan in less than 10 hours, stopping only to fill up the tank, stretch his legs, and grab food along the way. Normally he would have kept his car in the city and flown, but he needed the time to emotionally make sense of things. His mood matched that of the Lincoln Tunnel as he drove through it – yellow and distorted and bleak. As he passed the Ohio border into the Great Lakes state, Granger was beginning to see his breakup as an opportunity in disguise.

By the time he was done helping Abby, he was downright optimistic.

As for Abby, after spending 12-hour shifts with doctors, many of whom were woefully lacking in social skills, it was a pleasure for her to be face-to-face with a person of the opposite gender who seemed genuinely interested in relating to her emotionally.

"So, what's your next move?" Abby asked with a half-grin creeping along her mouth.

"Well, here's the part where I say something witty, like 'that'll be $43.50, please.'"

"And then I take a moment to gather my thoughts together while searching my purse, all the time thinking, 'Gee, I hope that he asks me to grab a cup of coffee.'"

"Except that you don't have enough cash to cover, so you whip out a credit card, and I have to tell you that our credit card machine isn't working today."

"But to save me from being embarrassed, you offer to take whatever I have in my purse, so in exchange for your kindness, I ask you out for coffee instead."

"That's how it works?"

"Sure. It's the least I could do after stiffing you for $3.50."

Suddenly, Granger could feel the disappointment of a lost relationship lifting off him like a skid of bricks. "Finally," he thought. "I'm free to explore the possibility of an intimate relationship again."

He realized that his time with Becky had been the equivalent of thin ice formed on a lake. While it had been an adventure, there hadn't been any substance to it, and after a while, the unspoken frustration between them about not being able to go below the surface cracked them apart. He had no idea where this new friendship was going, but he wasn't afraid to pursue it, one step at a time.

Abby was thinking, "So this is what it feels like to have expectation pull trepidation out of the driver's seat!"

For her, it was nothing short of thrilling. In fact, she had to admit to the sensation of butterflies in her stomach. Something she hadn't experienced since high school, when Alan Severson, who had been incredibly good-looking but equally shy, had come out of his social shell long enough to ask her out to their senior prom. They had a great time together that evening, and Abby had been looking forward to being asked out again. However, Juliette de Riger had been a bit more aggressive in making her intentions known, and it was Juliette, not Abby, who then captured his interest.

Sometimes life can be thoughtlessly random, can't it?

Which is to say that it's difficult to predict where two human beings who initially like each other will wind up. While it's been said that opposites attract, it's also fair to mention that oftentimes, it's those very opposite things that wind up getting on people's nerves. After all, we're people, not magnets.

"I'd love to grab something hot to drink," Granger replied. "The lot closes in ten minutes."

Before you could finish singing "The 12 Days of Christmas," Abby and Granger were sitting down at Mama Mia's Café, which had nothing to do with Italian cooking or the Broadway play inspired by Abba's songs. In fact, the café was owned by Dolores Feinstein in a rebellious statement against her kosher upbringing. She was notorious for combining all sorts of ingredients that couldn't possibly be good for each other into wonderfully eclectic creations. For instance, her version of hot chocolate was a mixture of dark chocolate, half-and-half, with equal dashes of ginger and cayenne pepper.

Although it was way past the dinner hour, Dolores was still at the café, hard at work, offering lingering customers her homemade food along with all the advice she could get away with offering. Her steady patrons had come to see Dolores as a very wise woman, something of a cross between Dear Abby and Julia Child.

"What'll it be, you two?" Dolores smiled at Abby, who was one of her best customers and friends.

"What's good?" asked Abby, noticing that Dolores had no qualms about staring at Granger, as if trying to place him.

"Give up?" he asked her lightheartedly.

"Sorry, it's just that I usually can place a person if I think I've seen them before. And I know I've seen you, but it's just not working."

Granger laughed. "That's because I haven't been around much."

"Would you like a hint?" Abby chimed in.

"Sure. Otherwise, it'll be a long time before you'll get your orders placed."

"Think Christmas trees," she suggested.

Dolores frowned as she sat down next to Abby. "O.K., I'm drawing a blank with that one."

"Then we'll move on to ordering and come back," said Abby. "I'll take hot chocolate and some fries, please."

Granger only needed a second to look the menu over before deciding. "Michigan cherry decaf with whipped cream and nutmeg on top!"

Dolores made a mental note of the orders and headed to the kitchen. In 20 seconds, she was back at their table.

"I got it!" she said, looking at Granger intently. "Your parents run the Christmas tree lot just north of here. I always get my tree there. And you're Jerry and Molly's son. Granger, you really had me going there for a minute."

"That's me."

"What brings you back to town?"

"The ghost of Christmas past, I guess."

"Well, ghost or no ghost, it's really good to see you!" Dolores then got up, playfully rubbed his hair, and went off to take another order.

"She's a sharp one," said Abby. "What did you mean by the ghost of Christmas?"

"I already pretty much covered it," Granger began. "I had a steady girlfriend up until a month ago. Classic case of love's labor lost. How about you?"

"My line of work doesn't really promote an atmosphere of romance. I'm a critical care nurse. There are plenty of available guys at work, but they're available for a reason."

Granger furrowed his eyebrows. "Meaning?"

"They tend to steer clear of commitments. That way, they have time to concentrate on their careers."

"What about you?" he asked.

Abby found herself smiling at the question. "I love my work, but I'm not in love with it."

And just then, she got an image of Granger in her kitchen. He was helping to cut up vegetables for the dish she was making. They naturally moved around each other, almost dancing in between the stove and the sink and the cutting board.

"Do you like to cook?" Granger asked.

You could have knocked Abby over with a feather. "Of course!"

"How would you like to come over to my parents' place and help me cook up a pot of chili tomorrow?"

Abby's face lit up. "I'd like that."

Abby was all smiles as she picked up her cup of cocoa. "Here's to Christmas future!"

Granger lifted up his coffee. "God bless us, everyone!"

Dan Salerno

Ashley's Wish

Ashley turned off her DVD player in tears. "They just don't make movies like *The Apartment* anymore!" she said out loud, to no one in particular. "Where's a guy like C.C. Baxter when you really need him anyway?" referring to the insurance clerk portrayed by Jack Lemmon.

Only Ashley's closest friends knew of her favorite movie from 1960. The one where a very young, beautiful, and talented Shirley MacLaine showed flashes of brilliance as Fran Kubelik, the elevator operator who had an Achilles' heel for married men. Of course, an equally young and talented Jack Lemmon was no slouch as Mr. Baxter, her shining knight in a cookie-cutter two-piece suit.

Together, they played a pair of two restless, lonely Manhattan souls.

"But you live in Richland!" her best friend Mary reminded her. "This isn't the Big Apple. It's Michigan, and we don't take the subway in to work."

"I know that!"

"So why do you keep watching that terrible movie, and then I wind up helping you out of another funk induced by it?" Mary asked.

"Is that what you think this is?"

"I don't think it, Ash. I know it, for a fact."
"What makes you so confident about that?"
Mary looked Ashley right in the eyes. "Because I know how many times you've seen that movie!"
"How many?"
"At least a dozen times this year. Not to mention we've just started the two-weeks-to-Christmas countdown, so you know what that means."
"Please tell me."
"You're about to set a personal best for complete viewings of *The Apartment* in a single year. And that doesn't include scene-selecting your way through another good cry," said Mary.

Ashley narrowed her eyes, which she only did when she was about to come up with a bogus excuse for something that she knew was true. She had learned to do this by watching how her mom handled her dad. Whenever they were on the verge of having an authentic conversation about something, Mom gave him the squint-eye treatment. Her code for "I don't want to talk about it right now."

The trouble was, Ashley's mom *never* wanted to talk about it. So, one day, after an especially harrowing experience where the squint eye didn't have its effect, her dad packed a suitcase, kissed his daughter good-bye, and walked out the door. He figured it was a waste of time to say anything to his wife, so he turned to Ashley and said, "Honey, it's not your fault. Promise me you'll remember that."

To which a stunned six-year-old Ashley replied, "O.K., Dad. See you later," as he kissed her again before walking out the door. She had no concept of a parent leaving for good. In her six-year-old mind, she thought he was going to run a few errands and be home in time for supper. There hadn't been any sit-down discussion with either of her parents to cue Ashley in on the split-up. It didn't help that her father's walk-out happened one week before Christmas.

To be honest, Ashley's dad wasn't exactly a communications guru. It was a good thing that she had a great memory, because he wasn't around much to reinforce what he had told her. He moved out of Michigan to California shortly after the divorce.

"I can't help it if I'm a huge fan of Billy Wilder," Ashley said.

"He made other films."

"None as good as this one!" Ashley held up the DVD as if she were holding a rare gem worth millions.

"Aren't you afraid of ruining it by playing it so many times?"

"DVDs are practically indestructible. Besides I have a backup copy."

"There are better ways to deal with disappointment!"

"Like what?"

"Like joining a dating service or asking a friend to set you up with a date. Use your imagination!"

That comment got Ashley smiling. "I *am* using my imagination! Enjoying *The Apartment* and watching Mr. Baxter and Miss Kubelik interact. He is such a genuinely nice guy."

"Ash, that's because Jack Lemmon played him that way."

Mary rolled her eyes as Ashley continued. "He should have won the Academy Award. Shirley MacLaine, too."

Ashley and Mary had been best friends since grade school. Ashley attended St. Monica's in Kalamazoo because it was the closest Catholic school to Richland, about 11 miles south, transferring to Hackett High School to finish her K through 12 adventure.

It was a classic mixture of opposites being attracted to each other. Ashley was the product of a single-parent home.

She had grown up in Richland Acres Apartments, almost across the street from Richland Elementary, where Mary had begun her education.

Mary was the first child of four. She was adventurous, determined, independent, and very sociable. She had curly, auburn hair that ran wild on humid days in the summer when she spent most of the day outdoors. Mary had been born right before the proliferation of social media and online games. Being a tomboy, summertime meant endless rounds of pick-up soccer, basketball, and kickball with neighborhood kids.

Ashley, on the other hand, was curious but on the shy side. She always had the option of playing with other kids in the apartment complex she lived in and never wanted for companionship. The golden-haired, blue-eyed girl had loved reading, and after her parents' divorce, she tended to retreat into the comfort of books, mostly fiction, with the notable exception of the Bible. Take, for instance, the beginning of Genesis, which was one of her favorites:

In the beginning, God created the heavens and the earth. The earth was formless and empty, and darkness covered the deep waters. And the Spirit of God was hovering over the surface of the waters. And God said, 'Let there be light,' and there was light. And God saw that the light was good.

As many times as Ashley had read this verse, the sheer power of a being who called things into existence out of nothing never ceased to amaze her. This was someone who lived on a different plane than humans, or anything else on earth, for that matter. Secondly, she was in awe of a being who took the time to express pleasure at what they had created.

Purposeful, deliberate, and joyful, thought Ashley. How else would you explain the summation of the creation of the earth a few verses later?

Then God looked over all he had made, and saw that it was very good... So the creation of the heavens and the earth and everything in them was completed. On the seventh day, God had finished his work of creation, so he rested from all his work. And God blessed the seventh day and declared it holy, because it was the day when he rested from all his work of creation.

This was no passive creator who set things in motion and stood idly by, waiting for an existential playing out of fate. This was active involvement from the very beginning.

"Ash," said Mary, bringing her friend back to the conversation. "You have that look in your eyes."

"What look?"

"The look you get when you're about to drift off into never-never-ever land!"

Ashley couldn't help laughing. "And where would that be?"

"Someplace Google Earth hasn't tracked down yet."

Another difference between the two friends was that one was trying her best to follow a semblance of moral order from a spiritually grounded base. The other saw religion as just another phase that the human race went through on its way to enlightenment. Mary believed that God (as a cosmic force) existed inside every person. Ashley held the view that God (as in a supreme supernatural being) also existed independently from us.

"Believing in God has very practical applications," said Ashley to her doubting-Thomas friend.

Their mid-December conversation was influenced by Ashley's own experience of the holiday. For her, it was the remembrance that her father had left the family during a season that was supposed to be marked by joy and peace. Her mom had sent Ashley to St. Monica's for the purpose of offering her daughter some spiritual stability. At home, there were massive amounts of love shown to her daughter to reinforce any lessons learned in school.

Ironically, when Ashley tried to explain this to Mary, it fell on deaf ears. When agitated enough, Mary countered with her own logical arguments. Most fell under the "Why does God allow bad things to happen to good people?" category. There weren't any philosophy classes offered in middle school, but even so, Mary probably wouldn't have been emotionally able to relate to the pure logic of it all.

"Pardon?" Mary asked.

Ashley laughed before picking up the conversation. "You know what your basic challenge is?"

"I'm dying to be told!"

"You're so full of fear of not being in control that you don't have any room for faith to take hold."

Mary raised her eyebrows. "That's harsh!"

"Well, I'm sorry, but how many times have we argued about this exact same thing?"

"I can't help it if you're stuck in a religious rut."

"What rut?" Ashley asked.

"The rut that says there's an all-loving, all-powerful, all-knowing God who is looking out for us."

"What if it's the truth?"

"What if it's not?"

"You're not asking the right question."

"So, am I just supposed to quit being logical so I can tune in to my spirit?"

Ashley smiled. "Exactly."

"I don't get you," Mary said. "You were slammed, big time, right before one of the biggest Christian celebrations of the year. I mean, right in the middle of the comfort and joy season, your dad took off. And it was never the same for you or your mom. But you soaked up all that religious hocus-pocus like nobody's business. It would seem that if there were a person who had an excuse for being an atheist, it'd be you."

"But you aren't an atheist," Ashley countered.

"Technically, no. I mean, there's a force inside us that draws us together."

"You're beginning to sound like a pint-sized Buddhist."

"Good and evil are a continuum of a circle of life, but most people are just too scared to admit it."

"Admit what?"

Outside, the snow was falling and seemingly, as if on cue, a group of carolers outside their apartment building began singing.

Silent night, holy night!
All is calm, all is bright.
Round yon Virgin, Mother and Child.
Holy infant so tender and mild,
Sleep in heavenly peace.
Sleep in heavenly peace.

Mary rolled her eyes. "That's exactly what I'm talking about. Those people, singing that song. I know they mean well, but it's total rubbish."

"That song they're singing has everything to do with why we celebrate Christmas," Ashley said, softening the tone of her voice.

Silent night, holy night!
Shepherds quake at the sight.
Glories stream from heaven afar.
Heavenly hosts sing Alleluia!
Christ the Savior is born!
Christ the Savior is born!

"Even if I gave you the virgin birth, how about the angels singing to a group of shepherds in the middle of nowhere? Why would God deliberately go out of his way to fool us by coming in the form of a baby born in a stable?"

Silent night, holy night!
Son of God, love's pure light.
Radiant beams from Thy holy face,
With the dawn of redeeming grace,
Jesus Lord, at Thy birth,
Jesus Lord, at Thy birth.

"I think that last chorus pretty much answers your question," said Ashley, sensing the confusion and anger that was buried inside her friend's heart.

Mary got up from across the living room. She had been sitting on the couch and she slowly stretched and sat down on the floor next to Ashley before going on. "Ash, I appreciate the depth of your imagination. I really do. But there is no pure light or radiant beams. Tell me, where's the redeeming grace?"

Ashley knew that her best friend had an amazing social conscience. From the time they were in grade school, whenever there was a canned good drive for the local food pantry, Mary had taken the lead in knocking on every door in their apartment complex. Later when there were protests against the latest military invasion, it was Mary who had convinced Ashley to join the demonstration. And when they were in high school, it was Mary who had motivated her to get involved in anti-human trafficking efforts.

"Why can't Mary see that God's behind all these efforts?" she wondered. Truth be told, when it came right down to it, Mary was a lot more active in doing good than many of the followers of faith that Ashley knew.

"What you're asking is why there is such pain in the world if such a good God created it?"

"I'm not even asking where the evil comes from; I'm asking why it's allowed to exist in the first place." Mary countered.

Ashley paused. Her thoughts were interrupted by yet another carol being sung.

Joy to the World , the Lord is come!
Let earth receive her King;
Let every heart prepare Him room,
And Heaven and nature sing,
And Heaven and nature sing,
And Heaven, and Heaven, and nature sing...

"I just don't see where the joy is coming from. I really don't." It was Mary now who seemed to be in some sort of self-induced funk. It didn't help matters that she had spent the years after graduating from college working as a medical social worker at a local hospital. She had seen firsthand how severe illness seemed to expose what was at the center of a person's life. As she gathered case notes, it never ceased to amaze her how people of strong faith seemed to cope the best. It was a continual source of frustration that their faith could not be her own.

Ashley sat closer to her friend. "I can't begin to answer why evil is allowed without bringing in the aspect of faith. Otherwise, I'll sound delusional to you."

No more let sins and sorrows grow,
Nor thorns infest the ground;
He comes to make His blessings flow
Far as the curse is found,
Far as the curse is found,
Far as, far as, the curse is found...

Mary slowly shook her head. "It seems like the thorns are winning nowadays. At least from where I'm sitting. Or maybe I'm just too tuned in to the amount of pain and suffering that's around me. You know what Buddhists say about that."

"No, I don't."

"A Buddhist would say that the first step towards enlightenment is to realize that life is suffering."

"I'm not denying that there is suffering in life."

"Then how can you be so naive?" Mary said.

"How can you be so hopeless and yet remain so socially active? It's contradictory."

"It's not contradictory. It's being a full-fledged human being, caring for others."

Ashley gently took her friends' hand. "It's being spiritual."

The melody of another ancient song came through their window.

O little town of Bethlehem,
How still we see thee lie!
Above thy deep and dreamless sleep,
The silent stars go by.
Yet in thy dark streets shineth
The everlasting Light.
The hopes and fears of all the years
Are met in thee tonight...

As if receiving the song as a salve, Mary smiled. From deep within her spirit, she received the grace to open up and see the wisdom of her friend's outlook. The singers kept singing.

How silently, how silently,
The wondrous Gift is giv'n!
So God imparts to human hearts
The blessings of His heaven.
No ear may hear His coming,
But in this world of sin,
Where meek souls will receive Him still,
The dear Christ enters in...

Mary spoke: "So, you're saying that the problem isn't with God; it's with us?"

For her part, Ashley was in the middle of her own personal revelation. In her mind she fast-forwarded through *The Apartment* to the scene where C.C. Baxter finds Miss Kubelick passed out in his living room, from an overdose of sleeping pills. Miss Kubelick needed someone to care about her. She needed a savior. It hit Ashley like a ton of bricks. It wasn't romance that Miss Kubelick was after. It was a relationship!

"Yes," she said as she got up off the couch. "That's exactly what I'm saying."

Ashley picked up the DVD she had been watching when the conversation began, walked to the trash bin in the kitchen, and threw it in.

Mary's eyes went wide. "Wow!"

"Yeah. Here I was asking you to take a gigantic leap of faith, while I was still relying on Jack Lemmon to get me through the holidays."

"Wow."

Ashley laughed. "You already said that."

"So, the bottom line is that I was using my social consciousness to override a belief in a personal God?" Mary asked.

"I don't know that the two are mutually exclusive."

"I was ignoring the spiritual dimension of it." Mary paused a moment to collect her thoughts. "But you want to know the curious thing about all this?"

"What's that?"

"We've had this conversation a hundred times before. But until tonight, I really couldn't see things from your point of view."

"Neither could I. You're a great friend for putting up with me."

Mary shook her head. "That's exactly what I was going to say."

Dan Salerno

At the Odeon

Jess was standing in the lobby of the Odeon Theatre, waiting to purchase his ticket for the 7:30 showing of *It's a Wonderful Life*. Meanwhile, there were probably 30 people lined up. Which, by big-city standards wasn't a lot, but for Kalamazoo, it was the equivalent of a flash mob.

It was a week before Christmas, and Jess had been stood up by his best friend, Angel, who had double-booked himself at a staff holiday party by mistake. The party was mandatory if you wanted to stay on good terms with your superiors, and since Angel had advanced to a mid-management position, he figured it was best to be there.

Meanwhile, here was Jess, with both hands in his pockets, trying to look friendly. He was 38 and short through no fault of his own. A ready smile and warm laugh more than made up for the lack of height.

As he waited in line, drinking a cup of hot chocolate, he was bumped from behind by an overly enthusiastic woman who could only be described as auburn-haired and extremely apologetic.

"I am so sorry!" she said while turning to face him. "I was trying to pull my mittens off and..." Her eyes went down to Jess' right foot, noticing the dark brown stain on the floor, inches away from his boot. "I am so, so sorry!" she repeated, biting her lower lip.

Jess followed her eyes down. "Hey, no harm, no foul."

She only shook her head in another attempt to apologize.

"I mean it," he said, smiling, noticing her bright blue eyes as he held out his free hand. "It's the price we sometimes pay for drinking chocolate in public... I'm Jess, by the way."

"Susan," she said, accepting his hand. "I'm not usually this clumsy, but..."

"Christmas brings out the klutz in you?"

She laughed. "Not really."

"You were reminiscing about Rudolph and got out of control?"

"Hard as it may be to believe, reindeer don't give me heart palpitations, although I do admit to atrial fibrillation now and then."

Susan was a medical transcriptionist, and even outside of work, she was fascinated with the terminology of her profession. She had never met most of her clients, who were surgeons. They communicated via email with voicemails attached. She typed up the notes and emailed them back, for which she was well paid. After all, without the transcribed notes, insurance reimbursement wasn't possible.

Jess worked as a graphic artist for the MLive group, which had bought out the *Kalamazoo Gazette* a few years back. Instead of working for one newspaper on-site, he now worked for three of them from home. It was a short commute, but the hours were long.

It turned out that Susan had also been stood up by a friend whose little girl was fighting the flu like a trooper but needed some TLC just the same.

Of course, Susan understood, not because she had kids of her own but because she was extremely empathetic, fueled by an active imagination. Even though she earned her income through science, she wasn't really the scientific type. She was left-handed, but right-brained. Somehow it all balanced out in that she was very practical, especially when it came to money. Her version of the perfect shopping experience was finding something in her size at the Salvation Army Thrift Shop that had only been worn a couple of times.

"So, how is it that you're standing in line by yourself, if you don't mind me asking?" Jess wasn't so much nosey as he was genuinely curious as to why such a beautiful woman would be going to any social function by herself.

"My friend couldn't come because her daughter's sick," she explained. "And I didn't have the energy to call anyone else. Besides, *It's a Wonderful Life* is my favorite movie, and how often do you get to see it on the big screen?"

"Why is it your favorite?"

'The scene where George Bailey finally realizes that he loves Mary Hatch while sharing the telephone with her. I must have seen it a hundred times, but it still knocks me out. Such beautiful, utter warmth. Don't you just love the way Mary totally ignores George when he rattles on about how he wants to get out of Bedford Falls? In my humble opinion, no other movie scene captures female intuition like that."

"Frank Capra nailed it, huh?"

"You mean, Donna Reed nailed it! With a little help from Jimmy Stewart."

"He was actually a little nervous about that kiss. It was his first movie since being back from World War II, and he was..."

"A little out of practice?" she said.

"Yeah," Jess smiled.

"But any actor would have given their right arm to kiss Donna Reed. She was so..."

"All-American?"

This time Susan smiled. "I was going to say wholesome, but then who's going to argue about such a gorgeous actress?"

The first time that Jess had seen *It's a Wonderful Life*, he had been on an initial date with Eileen, who had recently assigned her on-again, off-again boyfriend to the permanent off position. In a word, she was in no condition to be going to any type of movie espousing human kindness, especially one centered around the holidays.

For his part, Jess had been a bit ambiguous himself, but curiously, as Eileen started to let out a series of sarcastic comments during the movie, they had the opposite effect on him. As the movie ended, she was laughing hysterically while Jess was wiping away the steady flow of tears. Needless to say, they decided to call it a night right then and there, forgoing dinner or seeing each other again.

And ever since, Jess made it a point to watch the movie every Christmas season. He preferred to see it in a theatre because of the heightened effect of the large screen and the catharsis of an audience reaction.

All of a sudden, Susan felt like steering the conversation towards a more personal level. "Do you normally start chatting with strangers standing in movie lines?"

"This is Kalamazoo," he smiled back. "How often do you find yourself waiting for more than a few minutes?"

"You didn't answer my question."

"Under normal circumstances, in a situation like this, I'd bring a book."

"What a shame."

"Why is that?"

"You could be missing out on meeting the love of your life by keeping your nose buried in a book."

Jess looked Susan full on. "Books don't disappoint."

In an instant, Susan had an image of being 14 in the Kalamazoo Public Library. She was roaming the 921 section searching for Dorothy Day's *The Long Loneliness*. Her religion instructor had mentioned that Dorothy, who had been a journalist for the American socialist press in the 1920s, had decided to leave her lover after converting to Catholicism. What made this decision particularly hard was that she had a baby with him while giving up her network of Bohemian friends.

Dorothy herself was to write of that period in her life: "I was lonely. Dead lonely. And I was to find out then, as I found out so many times, over and over again, that women especially, are social beings who are not content with just husband and family but must have a community, a group, an exchange with others..."

Susan also understood the power of commitment, which seemed to fly in the face of the way of the world, where everywhere you were pressured to pay attention to the latest trend almost to the exclusion of tradition.

Although the reflection took only a moment, she realized that she had left the conversation with Jess at a standstill.

"So, what book hasn't disappointed you lately?" she asked smiling slightly.

"*Waiting for God.*"

"Sounds ominous."

Jess laughed. "It's a collection of writings by Simone Weil. She was a very empathetic person for a philosopher. She really had a thing for what she called 'paying attention.' Really appreciating another person's experience. She wrote that 'every sin is an attempt to flee from loneliness.'"

You could have knocked Susan over with a feather. "You know, she could have been a good friend of Dorothy Day. She was one of the founders of the Catholic Worker movement during the Great Depression. A real stickler for social justice and peace issues."

"What do you think heaven is like?" he asked, changing the subject.

"Why would you assume that I believe in it?" she asked back, raising her eyebrows mischievously.

"Call it a wild guess, but your first choice of books was written by a Catholic, and most Catholics believe in an afterlife."

"And they are unfailingly polite," she smiled.

Susan held her arms out in self-defense. "You're good. Are you some sort of private detective?"

"No, I'm a graphic artist. How about you?"

"Medical transcriptionist who's in the game because I'm one of those rare birds who loved Latin."

It was Jess' turn to be impressed. "What was the attraction?"

"A huge percentage of the Romance languages evolved from Latin, not to mention medical terms."

Susan thought back to when she was a senior at St. Mary of the Lake High School. Sister Eusthus, the Latin teacher, was the only nun remaining of the teaching staff. One day, Sister had come up to her when Susan was at her locker, picking up books for the morning classes. There was a poster of Benny Goodman on the inside door.

"I'll be. Are you a fan of the Big Band era?" she asked.

"It's my favorite type of music," Susan told her.

Sister smiled and gave a tug at her habit. "Mine, too!"

She then nodded to Susan, looked at the clock mounted along the wall, and said, *"Tempus fugit,* young lady," before heading down the hallway.

"I was never good with other languages," said Jess. "But I do remember the old rhyme that kids used to mumble under their breath."

Susan looked him straight in the eyes and said, "Latin's a dead language, as dead as it can be. First it killed the Romans, and now it's killing me."

Jess smiled in response to the remembrance. He was the youngest of three boys. All through grade school, he had been teased by the kids looking at him and saying, "Hey, look! There goes 'My Three Sons!' How's Mr. Douglas doing?" and then breaking into the "My Three Sons" theme song that, thanks to TV Land, everyone in America now knew.

In middle school, the teasing gave way to girls mainly being focused on his older brothers, who were by then in high school and quite handsome, each having thick, wavy hair that was dark and matched their eyes. So, as far as they were concerned, Jess didn't have a chance, even though he also had the benefit of the family gene pool going for him. It wasn't until his senior year that Jess came into his own, with the added benefit of a confidence that came from learning how to roll with the punches combined with a great sense of humor.

Susan, although raised a traditional Catholic, now considered herself on the more liberal side of the stream, especially having discovered Dorothy Day at such a young age. She was a subscriber to *The Catholic Worker* newspaper and read it faithfully. Jess was your classic spiritual drifter, moving from Pentecostal to Baptist to Evangelical, all while toying with the idea of becoming a Quaker. He was searching, at heart, for a simple, genuine way to approach the Creator.

As the line inched up towards the ticket counter, Jess was aware that he didn't want the conversation to end, and he picked up where it had left off.

"I take it you were very good at Latin?"

Susan nodded in agreement. "But I had a hidden agenda."

"Really?"

"I was looking forward to insulting the stuck-ups to their faces without them having a clue."

"You were fearless!" he said.

"I was socially awkward."

"Did it work?"

"For a while, but being a smarty pants never truly makes up for a lack of social skills," she answered.

"But you strike me as being a very friendly person."

"I'm friendly enough given the right circumstances, but I'm not an extravert. Your classic case of being outgoing on the outside, but shy on the inside. How about you?"

"I used to be socially feral, but I haven't lived in the wild for quite a while now."

"And you're modest as well. Are your arms sore from having to chase all those women off with a stick?"

Jess smiled. He was enjoying this chance meeting very much, and his brain was working overtime to figure out a clever way to keep this encounter going. "No such luck, I'm afraid."

They were now only a few feet away from the ticket counter.

Susan decided to be bold. "What's your favorite Christmas memory?"

"That would be making horn cookies with my mom."

"What are they?

"My dad got the recipe from one of his sisters. His mom made them every holiday season. They have butter, flour, sugar, and walnuts in them, and you roll them up like a croissant. They're delicious. How about you?"

"Trimming the Christmas tree with my mom's old records playing. Like Rosemary Clooney, Andy Williams, Nat King Cole, and Johnny Mathis. It was great."

"What's your favorite Christmas carol?"

"That would be 'Good King Wenceslas.'"

For Susan, it summed up what the season was all about.

It was a story about a king and his page out on a cold winter's night who came across a poor man who had very little. In response the king asked his page to gather food and invite the man out of the cold to eat. The last verse summed up the story:

> *In his master's steps he trod*
> *Where the snow lay dinted*
> *Heat was in the very sod*
> *Which the Saint had printed*
> *Therefore, Christian men, be sure*
> *Wealth or rank possessing*
> *Ye who now will bless the poor*
> *Shall yourselves find blessing.*

"Interesting choice," said Jess. They were next in line to purchase their tickets.

Susan couldn't help but notice how she was responding to their standing-in-the-movie-line conversation. She usually didn't go to movies by herself. She hadn't intended to come to this one alone. But she was having a great time, and the movie hadn't even begun yet.

She wasn't one to step out too often and do something spontaneous. On the other hand, she had come a long way since using Latin to get back at her peers. She had learned that a little subtly goes a long way. Jess, for all his creativity had learned a thing or two as well, like it's okay to step outside of your social circle every once in a while.

"Can I make a suggestion?" she offered. Susan could hear the beating of her heart. It felt like a freight train going full steam along a straightaway. She was living proof that you can be subtle and still be scared.

"Feel free."

"Since both of us are about to sit alone, why not sit next to each other?"

Now she'd gone and done it! There was no turning back now. It was a 'yes' or 'no' situation with no way of declining without a ton of awkwardness descending on them. Why couldn't she have left well enough alone, for crying out loud?

Susan realized she had been holding her breath and was about to faint. So she let it out and relaxed.

For his part, Jess was offering up a silent prayer of thanksgiving. He was no fool and understood completely how fate was smiling down on them both. How often do you meet such a likable person standing in line while you're waiting to see your favorite holiday movie?

Frank Capra, who directed *It's a Wonderful Life*, was surely smiling down from heaven to see that one of his films was being used as the backdrop for this moment.

Jess smiled broadly, affirming Susan's idea.

"Merry Christmas," she said, smiling back.

"Merry Christmas!" he said as they walked into the theatre together.

Comfort and Joy

After supper at her mother's home, Susan excused herself and went upstairs to the attic. Her mom had asked her to bring down the Christmas decorations so she could help her trim the tree. She was a no-nonsense kind of woman, mostly in response to growing up in a single-parent household.

Susan had seen firsthand the strain of being a single mom. Martha hadn't really intended on having a child, and the father hadn't wanted to be a father, so the split was mutual and for good.

Growing up, Susan remembered very little contact with her mom's side of the family. Martha had mentioned that there was a history of alcoholism that had gotten in the way of much solid communication. And however unintended her pregnancy, Martha had chosen to move in the direction of establishing a solid foundation for her daughter.

Christmas had always been a bit of a mixed bag. On the one hand, Martha was an agnostic. She had no formal exposure to God growing up, so her own belief system was cobbled together from skewed personal experiences that were never shared with anyone in hopes of keeping family secrets private.

This legacy was passed on to Susan who accepted it by osmosis. There was love and kindness shared between them, but it was not actively tied to any sort of religious belief. The result was that Susan was encouraged to search on her own.

Susan opened the attic door, easily finding the boxes marked "Christmas Decorations." As she knelt to open one of them, she found herself remembering the first time she walked into a church. It was the college chapel where she had a few minutes before her morning classes.

She was drawn to sit in a section that was flooded with sunshine coming in through the stained-glass windows. Soon after she sat down, a student sat across from her.

"First time?" he asked nonchalantly.

"Pardon?"

"Your body language is telling me you haven't been a regular."

Susan laughed at the reference to her unchurched status. "You're right. I've never been in a church before."

"How's it going, so far?"

"To be perfectly honest, you interrupted me."

"I'm sorry," he apologized. "I didn't mean to disturb you."

"I was on the verge of asking God something."

His wrinkled forehead indicated an unspoken question.

She nodded her head. "I was just about to ask, if God is intentional and we're supposed to be made in God's image, then why is it that the motivation for 99 percent of what we do as human beings is completely unconscious?"

The young man shrugged his shoulders. "Sounds like you've taken a philosophy class or two."

"Not really. I just read a lot and try to fill in the blanks on my own."

"So, are you asking me my opinion on the subject or inviting me to wonder along with you?"

She smiled. "You must be an upperclassman. I'd guess a junior."

"Why's that?"

"Because you're too quick on your feet to be a freshman, too cynical with strangers to be a sophomore, and not quite sharp enough to be a senior."

"Good guess, but maybe I'm just an unusually urbane newbie on campus."

She shook her head, "If you really were a freshman, you wouldn't be so quick to admit it. And yes, I was asking your opinion."

"Well, comparing humans to God is risky business. We may have a brain because God has one, but if there is a God, then God's brain has got to be way more sophisticated."

"That's a cheap shot."

"How so?"

"Because that's like giving God an excuse for being unapproachable and vague." She awkwardly stuck out her hand. "I'm Susan Berkowitz, by the way."

He extended his hand to complete the handshake. "Robbie O'Brien. Descendant of the O'Brien tribe, High King of Ulster."

She raised her eyebrows at that one. "Really?"

"Possibly," he said, turning his head away to stifle a smile, then turned back and looked Susan in the eyes. "Most likely not, but it sounds impressive, doesn't it?"

"And I'm a descendant of the lost tribe of Israel that took the shortcut through the desert once they got across the Red Sea."

"No kidding!"

"Yeah, we got tired of waiting for Moses, so we headed for Tel Aviv, settled down, and invented matzoh."

"What about cream cheese with lox?"

"That came after we invented bagels."

At that point, Susan realized that she was attracted to this fairly short, auburn-haired guy with freckles who was wearing pretty thick, wire-rimmed glasses. His eyes were deep hazel, and she noticed that they had gold specks in them.

For his part, Robbie was feeling intrigued at how easily they had struck up a casual conversation in a setting that usually inspired silence.

"I take it your family didn't go to synagogue much when you were growing up?" he asked.

"We didn't go much anywhere. I'm the daughter of an only child, and my biological father left us before I was born."

Instinctively Robbie winced. He came from an Irish Catholic family of six kids. He was the only boy. With a dad and mom who genuinely loved each other. Which had a huge impact on the kids, who were born two years apart from each other. From the moment of birth, Robbie, being the middle child, had been surrounded by sisters who doted on him. By five years of age, Robbie was, in turn, doting on his younger siblings. Even to the extent of changing diapers, which turned out to be quite a bonding experience because the O'Briens used the old-fashioned cloth type.

"I'm sorry about your dad," he said. "Very sorry."

"What's to be sorry about?" Susan said. "Sometimes life serves up curveballs, so you have to keep your eyes open, or you'll probably strike out."

"Isn't it a little tough to step up to the plate when you're barely able to pick up the bat?"

"What's that supposed to mean?"

"I mean, you were born into a family with no dad."

"Sure, but half the kids in America grow up in broken homes."

"I'm only trying to acknowledge that it must have been hard on your mom and on you."

Susan wasn't about to get into the specifics of her early life. Not with someone she had just met, in a chapel of all places. Being inside a place of worship was a foreign enough experience for her. Talking to some guy she didn't know, about personal things, was equally strange.

"You're a little snoopy." She didn't want to appear harsh, but sometimes being direct was the only antidote to unwelcome curiosity.

Lucky for Susan, Robbie was undeterred. Growing up in a houseful of sisters had taught him much about the opposite sex. Like their endless thirst for conversation. Highly verbal would be the term he would use to describe his upbringing. And you could be sure that there were no such things as secrets in the O'Brien family. Robbie also inherited a double dose of diplomacy skills, which came in handy whenever he had to dodge any drama stemming from his siblings.

"I don't mean to intrude," he answered. "But you strike me as a person who is itching to expand their emotional repertoire."

"Pardon?" Susan had gained very little knowledge of boys growing up. Her mom avoided the adult version of them, and she had followed her mom's example. The experience of her mother (that guys were prone to being unreliable) had been passed down intact. And there were neither generous uncles nor a lovable grandpa to help make up for that shortsighted reasoning.

Robbie slowly sat down in the pew in front of Susan. He reached inside his jacket and pulled out a handkerchief. "Here," he said, handing it to her.

"What makes you think I need this?" Susan began. To herself, she thought, "Who was this guy who went around interrupting people, asking personal questions, and then handing them hankies?"

"It's just a hunch."

Suddenly, Susan began to cry. She felt a childhood's worth of frustration with relationships rise to the surface, and it came pouring out of her. She sobbed as her shoulders shook from the effort. Robbie got up, slowly sitting down next to her. He reached out his hand to her, and Susan held on to it for dear life.

As she continued crying, Susan kept holding Robbie's hand. No other words were spoken between them until she handed him back his hankie.

"Thanks."

"Cloth handkerchiefs beat Kleenex hands down when it comes to tear absorption, don't you think?" he asked.

A smile slowly came to her face. "I honestly wouldn't know about that," she said, sighing.

"Really? From the wetness content of what you handed back to me, I'd say you were a superstar at crying."

Robbie knew enough to realize that people don't open up emotionally on command. It either happens or it doesn't. And nothing kills intimacy like expectations. But sometimes a little humor gets the ball rolling.

"I'm not one to turn on the waterworks. I mean, I hardly cry. Ever."

"Well, I'm honored to have shared this moment with you."

"Are you being sarcastic?"

"No. I'm being honest. I grew up surrounded by sisters, and crying was an everyday experience in my house. So, I sort of took it for granted. But, for you, that's not the case at all. It's a healthy thing to let it out." He paused, "So, are you okay now?"

Susan cleared her throat. "Not really." She took a quick look at her watch. "But I only have ten minutes to get to class."

"Me, too."

All of a sudden, Robbie found himself feeling awkward, which hardly ever happened when he was around a girl. The conversation was just starting to get interesting, but Susan had a point.

"I'm on scholarship, so I can't afford to skip classes," she explained.

Robbie nodded his head and smiled. "Well, it sure has been interesting to meet you, Susan Berkowitz."

She returned his smile as she got up to leave. "You, too, Robbie O'Brien."

They walked out of the chapel and went their separate ways.

As luck would have it, Susan never saw Robbie on campus again. At the end of the semester, realizing a larger university would be a better fit, she decided to see an admissions counselor who helped her transfer her scholarships to Western Michigan University. A year later, Robbie graduated and got a job with a public relations firm in Kalamazoo.

He was living in the same town that Susan was attending school, but over the same two-year timespan, she had been more than busy with her class schedule. After graduation, she had been offered a job as a second-grade teacher in Ohio. She took the job and had been there for five years, loving every minute of it.

There was something exciting about having a roomful of fresh faces each year, each child eager to launch into an adventure in learning. There was the camaraderie among the educators who were engaged in their profession. And there was the security of having each day's lesson planned out. No matter what else was happening in her life, Susan could count on the consistency of the classroom. It was a natural balm to the insecurity of growing up in a house with an us-against-the-world view. She relished the team approach used between classrooms that let her know she was never alone. She had the support of a wonderful principal as well.

All of this had caused Susan to blossom into a person who saw her professional career as an adventure. She was continually taking advantage of in-service trainings, and summers were spent at Ohio State working on her master's degree. It didn't hurt that her salary increased each year as her academic and professional credentials were strengthened.

Robbie, on the other hand, after four years of copyrighting work, had begun to submit freelance material to a number of 'religious' publications. Eventually he had built an impressive resume of published material that put him in a position to decide to go national. Which would mean he could focus on his creative writing and put the ad agency work behind him.

Back at her mother's home, Susan took the first box of Christmas ornaments downstairs. In no time, she had gotten the other two boxes down and sorted them out. There was only one crucial ingredient missing.

"Honey, would you be an angel and go to Meijer and pick up a few strings of lights for the tree?" her mother asked.

Susan bundled up, got in her car, and headed to the store. It was 8:30 in the evening, exactly two days before Christmas, but the seasonal department wasn't busy. In fact, there were only a few shoppers there, looking at what amounted to decoration leftovers. She immediately focused on finding lights. Within a few minutes, she felt the brush of another person as they leaned over to examine a collection of half-off items.

"Excuse me," he said.

"No problem."

"I'm notorious for waiting 'til the last minute," he said, almost jovially.

As he turned to stick out his hand for a handshake, Susan recognized the voice and the gesture.

She turned and faced him. "Robbie? Robbie O'Brien?"

"In the flesh, Susan Berkowitz!"

There was no way on earth that Susan was going to tell him that she had just been thinking about him less than an hour ago. What are the chances of something like that happening, anyway?

Susan still didn't believe in God, and she sure didn't believe in fate or anything remotely related to it.

"Wow!" was all that she could think of.

"Yeah, wow! What's it been, eight years?"

"Ten, but who's counting?" She smiled almost shyly.

"The last time we talked, you and I were in the chapel at Hope College."

"You interrupted my attempt to get alone with God."

"But we had a fantastic conversation."

"Yes, we did. But I was in a hurry, and I was a freshman, and new to the whole college thing, and I didn't have the brains to ask for your phone number."

"It's a lot of pressure being on full scholarship, isn't it?" he laughed.

"I always wondered what happened to you. I mean, I assumed you graduated, but what was life like after college?"

"Well, after our first and only encounter, I couldn't help but have a lasting impression of you, too. I knew you were smart enough to finish college, but what about your career?"

"I'm an elementary school teacher, and I love it. How about you?"

"I'm currently a so-so ad agency copyrighter, but a pretty good freelance writer."

She laughed. "You're conflicted?"

"Not really. I've been responsible and paid the rent and saved some money, so now I can leave the roost and go solo. But tell me about teaching. What do you like about it?"

For some strange reason, Robbie's innocent follow-up question caused Susan to slump right down on the floor, next to boxes of tinsel. She began to cry softly at first, but soon gained momentum.

Without hesitation, Robbie sat down next to her. "Why do I seem to have this curious effect on you? I mean, if I remember correctly, you told me that you don't cry very often, right?" He reached into his coat pocket and handed Susan a fresh handkerchief.

"I don't." She paused long enough to blow her nose. "I know you're not going to believe it, but the last time I cried like this was when I was with you."

"Do you want to talk about it?"

She slowly shook her head, but the tears came hot and heavy. And she started to tremble as she reached out to Robbie and buried her head in his shoulder. They just sat there for a minute until she was able to speak.

"I am so sorry," he said.

"It's okay."

"No, it's not. Here we are a few days before Christmas, and an innocent question causes me to turn on the waterworks."

"If you don't mind an objective observation, I would say that what you're experiencing isn't a voluntary response," he said.

"You're right. But this time I don't want to explain it away. I mean, we aren't in college anymore, and I don't have a class to get to." She looked directly at Robbie. "And for the life of me, I can't logically explain why I react this way with you."

"Well, the first time, you were caught off guard. I mean, you said you were looking for God. For a lot of people, that can bring up very heavy emotions."

"Tell me about it."

"And like you said, we're meeting again close to Christmas, the motherlode of emotional holidays."

"But I'm not a Christian. I don't even know if there's a god."

"You don't have to believe in God to be searching. As a matter of fact, most agnostics are really good at exploring. They just have a hard time committing."

"At least, we admit when we don't know something instead of acting like we do." She handed his handkerchief back to him.

Robbie stood up, offering his hand to Susan, and as she took it, she sighed. "I don't mean to come across as being cynical. But that was a bit of a cheap shot."

This time, Susan knew she didn't want to use cynicism to keep someone she was attracted to at arm's length. In a flash, she understood the deposit of her mom's DNA that had given her such a feral disinterest in guys. And now, with all the strength she could muster up, she made a deliberate decision to begin to break off that part of her past.

"So, what can I do to make your shopping experience a great one?" Robbie asked, smiling broadly, to let Susan know, beyond a shadow of a doubt, that he was on her side.

"I need to pick up two strings of lights. I'm helping my mom decorate our Christmas tree."

He bent down and picked up the two boxes nearest him. "Will these do? Our buyer went all the way to France to get them."

"I didn't know this store sent their buyers out of the country. Aren't they on a local-market kick?"

"Normally that's true, but Christmas comes only once a year."

Susan felt herself trusting this guy she had met only twice. There was an undeniably strong connection between them.

"Would you like to grab some coffee?" Robbie asked.

"You mean, as in, let's continue the conversation and see where it takes us?" she said.

"Panera's right across the street, and they make killer chocolate scones."

This time, Susan saw Robbie's invitation for what it was. A simple act of kindness, sparked by genuine affection.

"Yes, I'd love it," she said smiling, handing back his handkerchief.

Dillon

When he was a kid, you could smell the anxiety coming off Dillon like a fragrance. Only the aroma wasn't exactly appealing.

He had spent most of his childhood reacting to it, but as an adult, he had learned not to make it his emotion of choice.

Dillon had developed a deep love of nature that had brought him to Barry County in Michigan, a place with rolling hills that reminded him of his home state of Kentucky. He had found a fisherman's cabin off Cloverdale Lake to rent while he went house-hunting.

So, early one morning, when he heard a car edging up his gravel driveway, the door open, and the soft swishing sound of a piece of paper being pushed under his front door, Dillon was somewhat annoyed. But curiosity got the best of him, and he got out of bed, putting on his flannel shirt before retrieving the piece of brightly colored paper.

"You are cordially invited," it cheerfully began, "to our Annual Christmas Dinner at St. Francis of Assisi Church in Orangeville." The other details, like the day, time, and directions, were included in smaller font at the bottom. There was a picture of St. Francis superimposed with Santa Claus in the background.

"Good grief," thought Dillon. "What kind of place is it that combines a guy like Francis with a guy like Santa Claus?" On second thought, Dillon didn't exactly have the skill set of a head chef, and the possibility of a home-cooked meal sounded tempting.

The only thing that stood in the way was his awkwardness in social situations. From the time he was little, Dillon had struggled with it. Partly because his mom and dad had split when he was seven. Which is an odd time of life to do something so drastic. You figure, by then, all the essentials, like toilet training and learning to walk and eat on your own had been covered, and the rest was gravy. Evidently, his parents hadn't been on the same page he was. Being an only child, Dillon didn't have the benefit of older or younger siblings to tell him that his conviction that he had somehow caused his parents' breakup was false.

Besides the guilt, Dillon was stuck with the insecurity of it all. If you couldn't trust the first two major adult figures in your life to stick together, then who, for God's sake, was reliable? He had spent his life searching for the answer to that one. No other relationship involved pledging before witnesses that you would be faithful to each other and, by default, to any other family members that should happen to be added.

So here he was, a mildly sarcastic 40-year-old, holding an invitation to a community dinner celebrating the season of God's Son coming to earth. As far as Dillon was concerned, there hadn't been much evidence of it.

Meanwhile, after dropping off the flyer, Maria had pulled her car out of Dillon's driveway and was headed to St. Francis Church. The dinner was that afternoon and there was lots of cooking to be done.

She was 38 and had never found the time to marry. For one thing, she had gone to Michigan State University to earn a Master's degree in Social Work, which had come in handy working for the Commission on Aging (COA). Technically, Maria hadn't needed the master's degree for that particular job since she was more focused on helping senior citizens in a rural setting than looking at her position as a career move.

A typical day for her started at seven in the morning. As the director of the COA, she really didn't have to be there when the kitchen manager came in to start meal prep for the lunch program, but she used the downtime to do some grant writing for additional activities. If there was anything that Maria had learned in her 15 years at the COA, it was that baby boomers (who were now seniors) were very focused on service delivery and they voted in a much higher proportion than the general population. Keeping this in mind came in very handy whenever the senior millage came up on the ballot.

For her, helping to prepare the annual Christmas dinner was a respite from the workday world, and it was a mission of pure joy. It was no wonder that Maria had a huge smile on her face as she opened up the door of the church's fellowship hall.

"I got the potatoes started," yelled LaTrese from the kitchen. "They're almost all peeled and cut." LaTrese, a 211 dispatcher for the county, was Maria's best friend. She had been married for 16 years to Doug Lehmer, who owned a sheet metal machine shop in Delton. They were both "people persons" and enjoyed helping others out. She was a notoriously early riser, so it was natural that LaTrese had gotten to the church first.

"Hey there!" Maria shouted back as she rounded the corner and came into the kitchen, eyeing the four huge turkeys that were ready to be put into the two large ovens. She took off her coat and got to work.

"How're the kids doing?" LaTrese and her husband Doug had twin girls who were teenagers and didn't get up on Saturday before 10 AM.

"Right about now they're dreaming about waking up," LaTrese responded. "How're things with you?"

By this she meant: How are things in the relationship department? This was always the topic of conversation when it came to finding out how Maria was doing.

"Well, I'm pleasantly in between engagements."

LaTrese raised her eyebrows before responding. "What's that supposed to mean?"

"I don't have a boyfriend at the moment, and it isn't bothering me," she smiled.

"You never seem to have a boyfriend!"

"And it doesn't keep me up at night. I just don't have the time. And anyway, 99 percent of the guys I meet happen to be a good 25 years older than me. I'm not looking for a senior citizen sugar daddy."

"You aren't getting any younger you know!"

"Neither is anyone else," Maria shot back.

"That's not my point, and you know it. You need to pay attention to your biological clock because one of these days it's going to quit ticking."

Maria's face exuded mock concern. "Good heavens! Then I had better place a personal ad in the *Hastings Reminder*, so that every eligible bachelor in the county can read it. How's this sound? Immensely eligible mom-to-be looking for the father of her potential children. Good teeth, good genes, and full head of hair preferred."

It was fortunate that this conversation was taking place at 7:30 in the morning, because Maria was also a morning person with a Type-A personality.

On the other hand, Dillon was not. After examining the flyer advertising the Christmas meal, he took a shower, got dressed and put some coffee on as he fixed oatmeal for breakfast. After eating, he pulled on his boots and coat to go for a bit of a walk to the lake. It was a clear day, and the northwest wind cut across making it crisp but not uninviting. He had glanced at the clock near the side door before heading out. It read nine o'clock.

As he walked, Dillon's boots made a crunching sound in the light snow that had fallen the night before. He looked down and noticed deer tracks headed to the water's edge. The outdoors had always appealed to him, mostly because there was no chance for pretension. The woods were the woods, and they were continually offering lessons to anyone who was wise enough to listen.

Dillon's wasn't a romanticized view of it all, yet he fully appreciated what Robert Frost had to say about the subject:

The woods are lovely, dark and deep,
But I have promises to keep,
And miles to go before I sleep,
And miles to go before I sleep.

To Dillon, the promises had to do with another of Frost's lesser-known poems:

God once spoke to people by name.
The sun once imparted its flame.
One impulse persists as our breath;
The other persists as our faith.

Dillon wondered, "Why is it that God, who could be so physically present in a burning bush to get Moses' attention, seemed to be so far away when it came to my life?"

Was this the dilemma that Frost was referring to by way of the 'two roads' in yet another poem?

I shall be telling this with a sigh
Somewhere ages and ages hence;
Two roads diverged in a wood, and I –
I took the one less traveled by,
And that has made all the difference.

Had Dillon's choices in life set him on the road "less traveled by" to the extent that God himself seldom went there? A Sunday school memory verse from long ago wriggled loose and shot straight ahead to consciousness, causing a laugh. Because the verse was out of Psalm 139, with David answering his own question about hiding from God's sight.

I can never escape from your Spirit!
I can never get away from your presence...

A few verses later David goes on to say:

You made all the delicate, inner parts of my body
And knit me together in my mother's womb...

It seemed to David that God was never very far away. And that God knew us better than we knew ourselves.

Regardless of where God was that day, Dillon knew it felt good to be by the lake. He had interviewed for the marketing position at Hastings Mutual Insurance over the phone and had been good enough to prompt a final in-person interview only a week ago. He had two weeks of vacation time accumulated from his last employer and had permission to use up the time before starting his new job. He was good at writing copy and knew how to handle social media. In between work assignments, Dillon had purposely chosen to limit himself to turning off his smartphone, checking voicemail periodically, and keeping his laptop offline.

His people skills were very good at the workplace, but outside the office was another story. It was no surprise that he wasn't in any type of serious relationship.

Maria, however, was a hands-on people person. Most of her day was spent in the presence of others at work and then off the clock, at church functions, community events, or in her neighborhood, which was a short walk away from Pennock Hospital.

It was getting close to 10 AM when she and LaTrese finished checking on the turkeys.

"Beautiful!" LaTrese commented as she and Maria basted them a final time.

"Less than an hour, tops." Maria smiled as they put them back in the oven and turned towards Maren and Madeline, LaTrese's twins, who had just walked through the kitchen door with their dad.

"Hey, girls! Hey, Doug!" LaTrese said, her face exploding with happiness. "How about setting up the tables while we finish up in here?"

In no time flat, the tables were set, with other folks coming in to put the final touches on the Christmas decorations that had been set up the night before. Someone put on a Christmas CD to set the mood even further.

"So, tell me, when was the last time you actually went on an official date?" asked LaTrese, as she mixed the canned corn with lima beans to make succotash.

"Right there's your problem," said Maria as she mashed the potatoes, using half-and-half with the milk to make them creamy white. "You tell me I've got to keep my eye on my biological clock, but that's not exactly a real creative way to nab a guy."

"Good grief!" LaTrese sighed in mock frustration. "That's not what I meant, and you know it!"

"I told you, I'm open to advertising in the newspaper."

"You don't need an ad. You need a lifestyle change," said LaTrese.

"Should we rob the Shell station and turn over a new leaf together?"

LaTrese couldn't help but laugh.

Underneath the good-natured ribbing, LaTrese's point was well taken. Maria had often wondered how much of her busy schedule was simply a cover-up for not wanting to bother with the logistics of managing the possibility of a romantic relationship. After all, working for a nonprofit was an excellent alternative to admitting loneliness. At least during the day. Many evenings Maria had come very close to admitting it'd be nice to have someone to come home to besides Tiger, her cat.

It was almost noon as Dillon walked back into the cabin. He took another look at the flyer and noted the time of the dinner, which was scheduled to start at 12:30 PM. He had time to take a quick shower, change his clothes, and head to Orangeville, using the directions on the flyer to guide him.

He chose a deep green pullover sweater along with relatively new jeans. Dillon chose his clothes for quality and comfort, not for show. He figured the community meal wasn't meant to be a fashion showcase.

On the ride to the church, he found himself remembering the story of how St. Francis turned his back on his privileged upbringing to minister to the poor. It didn't hurt that Francis also had a heart for animals. Something that Dillon and the Saint had in common. "If only people could be as reliable as animals," he thought.

While his mind was on the subject, he made a mental note to himself to be sure to adopt a cat or two from the local animal rescue organization once he got settled into his new job. Two years ago, he had put a pair of cats to sleep within a few weeks of each other due to illness. The process had devastated him because he had gotten the pets (a couple of six-month-old felines who had grown up together) soon after moving out on his own from college, and they had been his constant companions ever since.

It was 12:28 PM when Dillon's Honda Fit pulled into the church parking lot, which was almost full. He felt his heart rate increase as he headed towards the church. But any awkwardness was soon put to rest when he opened the door. He was greeted by LaTrese, who was now filling the hostess position as other members of the set-up crew had taken over putting the meal on the tables.

"Welcome to St. Francis," she said, engaging Dillon with a warm smile and her bright green eyes.

"Thanks." Dillon managed a bit of a smile in response.

"I don't believe we've met. I'm LaTrese." She put out her hand, and he took it.

"I'm Dillon. Pleased to meet you."

LaTrese glanced down at his hands and noticed there wasn't a wedding ring. "So, will your family be joining us today?"

"No. I'm not married, and I don't have kids."

Her face positively lit up at Dillon's reply. "Well, then, I know just the spot to seat you! Follow me!"

He had to practically run to keep up with LaTrese. She walked right up to Maria and sat Dillon down next to her.

"Maria, meet Dillon," she purred. "Dillon, meet Maria." As he sat down, LaTrese flashed Maria a wink and quickly walked back to the front door.

"This is going to sound like a pick-up line," Maria said, "but you're not from Barry County, are you?"

Dillon couldn't help but laugh. "Why does everyone I meet wind up asking me that question?"

"Because it's a very small place and we tend to know each other, especially around Orangeville."

He also couldn't help but find Maria's amazingly black eyes attractive. Her mother's Hispanic heritage really blessed her with warm features, including equally black hair.

"I'm from Paducah, Kentucky. But I've lived in a lot of places since I left home."

"So, what brings you to our neck of the woods?" she asked.

"A job with Hastings Mutual. I'm in the marketing department. How about you?"

"I'm with the Commission on Aging, in charge of keeping our seniors healthy, engaged, and curious."

"Curious?"

"About life. Having something to look forward to. Always asking questions about what's next on the horizon."

"That's a pretty tall order, isn't it?"

Maria smiled. "Not if you look beyond the surface and see the gold. I absolutely love hanging out with seniors. Actually, I prefer their company to most of the adults my own age."

Now the cat was out of the bag! Maria had noticed that Dillon was munching on a celery stick like there was no tomorrow.

"Been a while since breakfast?" she teased.

"It must be all the food coming out of the kitchen," he began. "Actually, it's a coping mechanism I learned when I was a teenager."

Of course, being the people person that she was, Maria had no idea what he was talking about.

"I used to have a fairly good case of social anxiety," Dillon explained. "My mom sent me to a counselor who suggested that in situations where I'm uncomfortable, to focus on one small detail and let go of everything else that I can't control."

"I'm sorry."

"For what?"

"That someone or something hurt you so much that it bothers you to be in social situations."

"It only happens when I don't know anyone in the room.

"Then let me tell you three things I like about you, so we'll be friends," Maria replied.

Dillon was in no position to argue, so he smiled before giving his assent.

Maria smiled back. "First of all, you're a very interesting individual. Second, you have an honesty about you that's disarming. And third, you smell like Ivory soap."

A smile began on Dillon's face and kept on growing until he positively lit up. "It's my turn," he said.

She nodded her approval, moving a little closer.

"First, you have a genuine love for others. Second, you don't have a pretentious bone in your body. And third, you're very engaging and easy to be around."

Maria lifted her glass toward Dillon for a toast. "Friends?"

Dillon picked up his glass and gently touched Maria's. "Friends."

And as they toasted each other, the grandfather clock in the fellowship hall chimed.

Dan Salerno

Estabon

Estabon was sitting in the Kalamazoo Transportation Center, trying to decide if he was going to call his parents to let them know he was coming home for the holiday.

He had emailed them a week ago, letting them know that he was trying to get time off from his job as a waiter at an Italian restaurant. The manager had okayed his request, but now that he was sitting in the station, he wasn't so sure it was a good idea.

There were at least a dozen good reasons he could think of to simply get up and walk out the door before purchasing his ticket for the 10:25 Amtrak to Chicago.

He wasn't feeling all that close to his family. It wasn't too late to call his boss back and get some extra cash from holiday tips, which tended to be very generous. He didn't especially like traveling by train. He wasn't overly fond of Evanston. He hadn't seen his parents in three years. He was not especially in a holiday mood.

The bottom line was Estabon felt stuck.

If he continued to ignore his parents' requests to visit, he risked further alienation. If he responded to them, he risked offending them further than he had already.

It didn't help matters that he was the oldest child in a Hispanic family with a culture that placed great emphasis on family and obedience.

Mateo and Gabriela Sanchez were excellent parents. They loved their four children fiercely. Estabon's earliest memories included Gabriela making favorite meals for each of the children's birthdays. And Mateo's almost constant grin when boasting about his children before others (but never in front of the kids). It wasn't lack of love that held Estabon back.

"Why can't I just get over it? Where is this conflict coming from?" he thought, looking at the clock on the station wall. "It's two days before Christmas. I should be looking forward to spending time with my family!"

Estabon's mind raced backwards, taking him to when he was fourteen years old. He had an apron on, helping his father chop up peppers, tomatoes, and onions for the salsa they made from scratch in their family restaurant.

Mateo was watching his eldest son at work.

"Estabon. Please, for the love of the Savior. Slow down before you chop off your fingertips."

"Papa, I need to get this done! I have track practice."

"Track practice can wait a few minutes. Do you want to go through the rest of your life with no fingertips?"

"No, Papa."

"Besides, you chop more evenly when you work a little slower. And remember, always chop away from you."

"Yes, Papa."

There was something about being the firstborn that automatically resulted in higher expectations. Estabon felt the pressure but couldn't talk to his father about it.

One glorious spring morning, right after he had mopped the restaurant's entranceway and helped his mother take the chairs off the dining room tables, Estabon paused a moment.

"What a beautiful day it is today!" Gabriela had opened the conversation, smiling at her son. "You know, your father, he loves you so much! He is so proud of you."

You could have knocked Estabon over with a feather. "He sure doesn't show it."

"How could he? He's a man. And he's your dad. And he isn't used to expressing what is going on inside here," she pointed to her heart for emphasis.

"I wish Dad would just lighten up sometimes, Mom."

"He means well."

"I know, but what he says, how he acts towards me. Sometimes it hurts."

"You're the firstborn," she tried to explain to him. "All the expectations, the fears, the learning what it is to be a parent – all of that gets put on the first child."

Estabon sighed in frustration. "It's not like I filled out an application to be the first one, Mom."

"Son, that's logic talking. Culture is not about logic. Let me tell you something."

She sat down and motioned for Estabon to join her.

"When your father was ten, his father took his wife and six children out of Texas to Chicago. He was tired of working the fields, and his cousin, Lupe, offered him a job in his restaurant. It was nothing special, but it was a start. All your father's siblings, one after another, worked at that same restaurant. They worked hard, and eventually opened another location, and were very successful. Your grandfather ran that other restaurant eventually."

"Dad's already told me as much, Mom."

"What he didn't tell you was the price he paid. No sports. No after-school activities. It was school, homework, and then walking to the restaurant to work until bedtime. None of your father's brothers and sisters had that schedule. Because he was the oldest. So, your grandfather taught your father and ran him very hard."

"I guess I didn't know that part, Mom."

"Your father would never have told you. He isn't one to complain."

"But I'm not like him, Mom! Can't he see that?"

"He sees an oldest son who he wants, very much, to see running his restaurant before giving it over to him."

"I'm 14, Mom. Don't I get a chance to live a little and decide later on?"

"Decide what?"

"If his restaurant is a good fit for me."

"Good fit?"

"If it's what I'd like to do with my life."

Gabriela smiled and moved closer to her son. "In our family, we don't look to see if something's a 'good fit' before we commit to it. We just see what needs to be done and do it. You should know better than that."

"Mom, we're in America. We have choices."

"I never said you didn't have choices."

"But it sounds like you've already decided what the rest of my life is going to be like, and I'm not even out of high school."

"It's not about choices, although you have them."

"Then what's this all about?" Estabon had to wipe the sweat off his brow he was so angry.

"It's about honor."

Estabon sighed in frustration. "Mom, I'm not trying to dishonor the family. But I'd like to decide some things for myself."

"I understand that, Son. But meanwhile, we have a very successful restaurant to run. A family business that pays for the home we live in, and the clothes we wear, and the food we put on the table."

He looked his mother in the eye. "What if I'm not cut out to be a cook? Maybe there's something else out there for me."

"God knows you best, son."

When Estabon was six, he fell out of a backyard tree. He had underestimated his reach while moving from one branch to another, more appealing one, a few feet higher up. In a matter of a few seconds, he had slipped down and was flat on his back, looking up at the sky. Luckily, he had fallen onto a huge pile of leaves that cushioned his descent.

Other than experiencing the peculiar feeling of having the wind knocked out of him, he was none the worse for the wear. "See how God protected you!" His mom had said as she held him close.

"If God was so great at protecting me, I wouldn't have fallen," he had said to Gabriela.

"Don't say such things!"

"Mom, it was the leaves that protected me. I was lucky; that's all."

"And who made the leaves?"

"The tree."

"And who made the tree?"

"It came from a seed that another tree made."

"Who made the seed then?" Gabriela was having a hard time hiding her frustration.

Estabon only rolled his eyes, sensing there wasn't going to be a winner in this conversation.

"It came from God." His mother's hands gently framed his face. "Every good thing comes from God."

"What about smallpox and measles, and all those other diseases. Where do they come from?" His six-year-old mind was plenty sharp enough to ask one last time. "You can't take responsibility for the good without taking responsibility for the bad, can you?"

"I don't question God, Estabon. You shouldn't either."

"Somehow, Mom, I think God's big enough to take it."

If only he could believe that now.

And now his memory took him back to his high school graduation. He had earned a 3.9 grade point average and was the third highest in his class in terms of academic excellence. This honor was even more significant, given that Estabon was working 15 to 20 hours a week at the restaurant at the time. He often took his homework to the kitchen with him, perched on a stool in between clearing tables and washing loads of dishes.

After the speeches had been given and the diplomas handed out, Estabon found his parents in the lobby of the high school auditorium. He expectantly walked up to them, a huge smile on his face.

"Way to go, Son!" Gabriela said, giving him a hug.

Estabon turned to his father, who solemnly shook his hand and took him aside.

"You should have finished higher," he whispered.

"What?"

"Weren't there two others ahead of you?"

"Yes, Dad, but..."

"I'm not interested in excuses, Son. If two kids finished ahead of you, then you could have done better, no?"

Estabon was crestfallen. So much so that he couldn't tell anyone else what his father had chosen to say to him on the night of his graduation. Although it had happened several years ago, that memory was always near the surface, eating away at his confidence.

Similarly, there were no congratulations coming from his father when he was accepted to Michigan State University on an academic scholarship that paid for three-fourths of his college costs.

His mother, of course, was ecstatic.

"Estabon, I am so very proud of you! This is proof that all that studying you did paid off!"

He smiled, showing the same acceptance letter to his father, who scowled slightly before handing it back to him.

"So, what do you think, Dad?" Estabon wanted to know what his father was feeling.

His father sighed. "I think if you had studied just a little harder, you would have gotten a full scholarship."

Four years later, Estabon graduated from Michigan State University with honors. The person who gave the commencement speech did a fine job telling the graduates, "Don't be afraid to pursue your dreams. Don't be afraid of falling down in the process. Just remember to get back up. And don't settle for anything less than your heart's desire. Because it's your heart's desire that's going to make a difference in the world."

"Well, you made it, Son," his father had told him. "But now you need to come home and work in the restaurant. Following your dreams isn't going to pay the bills now that you're an adult."

Two days later, Estabon packed his bags and moved to Kalamazoo, where he had a friend who told him he could get him a job at Caraba's as a waiter. He worked the evening shift, so his days were free to pursue his dream of being an artist.

Then there was Christmas, three years ago, the last time that Estabon had been home. It had started off fine until dinner on Christmas Eve. As was the tradition in the Sanchez family, each sibling went around the table, updating each other about what was happening in their lives.

When Estabon's turn came, he was eager to share.

"Well, I just had my first gallery showing."

"Estabon, that's wonderful," Gabriela said.

"What exactly does that mean, Son?" Mateo asked.

"Dad, it means that a gallery owner felt that my paintings were good enough to host a showing."

"A showing?"

"Where people could come in and see my paintings and buy them."

Mateo only shook his head in wonderment. "And you can make a living from these gallery showings?"

"Dad, it's a process. This was my first opportunity to show what I can do. It takes time to build up a following."

"I only hope you can continue to pay the bills while your following comes to you," Mateo said.

Thankfully, the subject was dropped, but the rest of the dinner wasn't quite as festive.

Estabon was still feeling the sting of his father's comment the next day as Gabriela drove him back to Union Station to get the train home.

"I am sorry for your father's opinion," she began. "He has no understanding of what it means to be an artist. All his life, your father has worked with his hands, very hard, to make a living for his family."

"I get that, Mom."

"He never had time for anything else but work. He doesn't see the beauty behind the paintings, Son."

"He doesn't seem to want to."

"It's not that he doesn't want to. He doesn't know how."

"What am I supposed to do about that?"

"Talk to him."

"I wish I could, but we've never had that kind of relationship. If we aren't talking about the restaurant, it's very hard to get him interested in anything else."

"His whole life is connected to the restaurant, Estabon, because when he sees the restaurant, he sees his family."

As Estabon now sat in the Kalamazoo Transportation Station, he still felt the frustration tugging at him.

The initial gallery showing of his work had slowly blossomed to include additional showings and even commissions to do work. He was making headway. He was scheduled to be part of a local artists' exhibit at the

Kalamazoo Institute of Arts (KIA). He was teaching a class at the KIA and mentoring young artists through the Hispanic American Council. But his father knew none of this.

From Mateo's end of things, he had initially been hurt when Estabon told him about being a waiter at Caraba's.

"Why would he move 250 miles away to do something that he could do here?" he asked his wife.

"It's in an upscale establishment," she told him.

"Upscale?"

"They cater to higher-end customers."

"Do they serve good food there?"

"Yes, it's very good."

"So do we. Authentic recipes that my great-grandmother used to make. What does this have to do with the kind of people who eat it?"

"Their customers can afford to pay more."

"We have always been a family business," said Mateo, trying hard to figure out what Gabriela was trying to say. "I see no reason why our son had to go outside the family to work at a restaurant so far away."

"It's more than that," Gabriela had said. "Our son is an artist."

"He couldn't be an artist in Chicago? This city is full of artists!"

"Sometimes you have to get away to establish yourself."

"By turning away from your family?"

Privately, Mateo had been proud of his son. Proud of him doing so well in high school and college. Proud of him making a go of it in Kalamazoo. Proud that his son had been responsible and paid off what little college debt he had without his father's help.

Whenever a customer asked about Estabon, Mateo beamed and told them, "My son is doing very well for himself. He's turning into quite an artist in Michigan."

Despite how he felt inside, Mateo could not fathom going against tradition to validate his son's life choices to his face. Like his son, Mateo, too, seemed to be stuck.

While Estabon was sitting in the Transportation Station, Mateo's father, Lupe, was having his own father-son chat.

"You are too hard on Estabon!" Lupe said, shaking his head as he helped cook up the tortilla chips.

"How could you say such a thing!"

"Because I see you, and I see how you judge him."

Mateo stopped chopping up tomatoes and looked his father in the eye.

"I was a good son to you, Papa. I obeyed you. I appreciated the example of hard work you gave me and the chance to eventually open my own restaurant."

"Yes, you were a good son. But I have to tell you something."

"What?"

"In some ways, you have been not-so-good as a father."

"Please explain."

"You know I love you. And I gave you my blessing on your hard work. That's the difference between you and me, and you and Estabon."

"You worked me hard, Papa, just like I tried to teach him. But I obeyed you."

"So did Estabon."

"No, Papa. He didn't."

"Mateo, just because Estabon didn't choose to work with you doesn't mean he disobeyed you. He learned to work just as hard as you did. He gave up a social life to work in the restaurant. He obeyed you. While he was working for you, he brought his schoolbooks here. I saw him studying here in this very kitchen. Night after night. He obeyed you by getting excellent grades and got a scholarship to college and graduated with honors."

"I know that, Papa."

"No, I don't think you do." Lupe put down the fryer, went over to his son, and put his hands on Lupe's face. "Your son needs you to bless him, not judge him. Yes, I taught you to work hard. Yes, I was hard on you. But I never, ever judged you."

Instantly Mateo began to weep, burying his face in his father's shoulder.

Lupe pulled his cell phone out of his pants pocket, handing it to Mateo.

"Now be a good father and call your son."

Mateo took the phone from Lupe, dried the tears from his face and punched in Estabon's number.

Estabon took out his phone from his coat pocket. He saw the call was coming from his grandfather, so he answered it.

"Merry Christmas, Grandpa!" he said, smiling.

There was a pause before the answer came from the other end. "Merry Christmas, Son. I'm so proud of you!"

Dan Salerno

Haley Goes to South Haven

Haley had just paid for her hot dog and chips at the North Side Memories deli. She walked across St. Joseph Street towards North Beach. Ahead of her was what she considered to be the most beautiful stretch of Lake Michigan.

It was just far enough away from the lighthouse to steer clear of the steady flow of folks who sought it out. And it was on the border of the private beaches. Usually there weren't very many people around–especially during the winter–which was her favorite time of year to go to the Lake.

That time of year, the water was more gray than blue, but it was peaceful and pristine. By the time late December rolled around, the waves had washed up enough water, mixed with half-frozen sand to form a chain of snow mountains along the shoreline, getting progressively higher as the winter wore on.

In winter, the beach looked almost extraterrestrial. It was hard to imagine anyone laying out on the shore, let alone going for a swim to cool off.

But to Haley, this was when Lake Michigan was at its best.

She was standing by the lookout bench about a mile up from the lighthouse, and as she finished up her hot dog, she put the wrapper in the trash and decided to go for a walk.

For some reason a scripture from Revelation came to mind: "I am the Alpha and Omega, the beginning and the end. Behold! I make all things new."

"How ironic," she thought. "How can God be the beginning and the end and yet make everything new?" If that were true, she certainly hadn't seen any of that freshness in her own life recently.

It had been 10 years since she'd had any sort of relationship with the opposite sex that could be called serious. Her relationship with Aaron had barely begun to go past the "just friends" mile-marker when he called her up to say he was moving out of state to take a new job. They were five years out of college at the time. She had begun to count on Aaron as the person she went to with her news of the day. Little did she know that the most significant of his own news was kept to himself.

Haley walked down to the beach and began to head north, where the shoreline soon became private beach, which meant you could walk on it but not lay down or swim.

She was a South Haven native, but many of the owners of the expansive beach homes were not. She grew up with a single mom who was a social worker for the State of Michigan. It was a steady job and paid the bills for the two of them, but it didn't leave much room for frills. If there was anyone who knew about the social undertow, it was her. Far beneath the surface were deep-seated challenges facing too many families that were just as dangerous as any sandbar.

As she started her walk, something from the second chapter of Proverbs came to mind, which was odd because she hadn't really spent much time with Bible study.

Tune your ears to wisdom,
and concentrate on understanding.
Cry out for insight, and ask for understanding.
Search for them as you would for silver,
seek them like hidden treasurers.
Then you will understand what it means
  to fear the Lord,
and you will gain knowledge of God.
For the Lord grants wisdom!
From his mouth come knowledge and understanding.
He grants a treasure of common sense to the honest.
He is a shield to those who walk with integrity.

She desperately wanted to understand and be wise!

Caught in her reverie, she didn't notice a stranger who was down on his knees, looking for stones, until she almost tripped over him. She had to hold onto his shoulders to keep from falling.

"Oh, I am so sorry!"

He laughed and stood up. "No problem. No hurt, no foul."

"I'm not ordinarily such a klutz."

"It's really not a biggie. This time of year, you'd hardly expect to come across any beachcombers."

"It's my favorite time to be out here," she said. "You have the Lake all to yourself most of the time, and the beach takes on a totally different appearance." She paused before continuing. "And I don't feel so guilty trespassing onto the private side of the Lake."

"But the shoreline is public. You can walk along here anytime you like."

She frowned. "Technically, that's true, but I still have to look at multi-million-dollar houses."

As soon as the words came out of her mouth, Haley turned beet red. When would she learn to stop judging? She couldn't help it. Her own home had been a small two-bedroom, less than 800 square feet, with a yard the size of the proverbial postage stamp. It was a testament to frugal living, if ever there was one.

"You know, money, in itself, isn't the problem. It's the love of it," the gentleman said.

"Unfortunately, it doesn't seem like you can have one without the other."

He chose to ignore the retort and instead held out his hand. "I'm Zach Stiller."

"Haley Malley," she said, shaking his hand tentatively. He was on the short side, and from outward appearances, seemed to be an outdoor sort of person. From the looks of his casual but elegantly styled clothes, she guessed his family was one of the many from Chicago who had summer homes on the other, quieter side of the Lake. In fact, Haley had guessed correctly. Zach's parents had moved to Elks Grove and ran their own public relations firm in the city. They were extremely successful and bought property in South Haven when it was relatively cheap, later building a house.

They knew the value of hard work. Their success hadn't been overnight. And they had made the land purchase and home their only major investment as Zach and his sister, Simcha, were growing up.

"I'm sorry for the remark about money," she told him. "Fact is, we didn't have much in my family, and I sort of resented those who did."

"Because they flaunted it?"

"Yes."

"But not everyone does that," Zach said.

"I know, but it seems that way."

"You know, Jesus had a lot to say about how to treat the poor."

She had to bite her lip a bit before responding. Haley was a semi-lapsed Catholic, the kind who only went to Mass on Christmas and Easter. And then, it was mostly out of an odd mixture of habit and guilt. She had gone to public school growing up.

"Why would you say that?" she said, taking a neutral stance on the subject.

"I read the Bible along with the Torah in my comparative religion class in college," he said. "I absolutely love what Jesus had to say about the subject."

Haley was stumped. "Like, for instance?"

"Well, how about this from 1 Samuel? *The Lord raises the poor from the dust and lifts the beggar from the ash heap, To set them among princes and make them inherit the throne of glory.*' Or Psalm 22, '*The poor shall eat and be satisfied;*' or Psalm 41, '*Blessed is the person who considers the poor, The Lord will deliver them and keep them alive.*' Or Psalm 69, '*The Lord hears the poor.*'

"Remember what Jesus said that day when he opened the scripture scroll and read in the synagogue in Capernaum?" Zach asked.

She shook her head.

"He said he had come to preach good news to the poor!"

"How is it that you know so much about Jesus?"

Zach smiled. "Jesus was Jewish. His whole life was spent immersed in his own culture, which was Jewish."

"I'm sorry. I didn't mean to criticize your ethnicity."

"What do I do now?" she thought. Haley hadn't meant to bump into such a philosophically minded person. She had come to the beach that day because it was sunny, and she wanted to clear her head. Christmas wasn't much of a holiday for her. Growing up, there hadn't been extra money to spend on frills. She had gotten into the habit of ignoring most of the materialism that surrounded the holiday, but her heart was still searching for some alternate meaning.

"The problem is, intentions aren't enough," he continued.

"How so?"

"There has to be follow-up. You're familiar with what Micah said on the subject, right?"

"Not really."

"He wrote, 'What does the Lord require of you? To do justice, love mercy, and walk humbly before the Lord your God."

To be sure, Zach hadn't headed for the beach searching for an opportunity to wax poetic about social justice or anything else. He was visiting his parents, home for the holidays, trying to sort things out as well. Only it wasn't anything theological. It was in the relationship department that he needed a tune-up. Reason being, he worked as a graphic designer for a marketing firm back in the Windy City, and he was on the social engagement committee of the reformed synagogue he attended, which meant when he wasn't at work, he was helping to plan some sort of outreach linked to peace and justice issues. It hardly left time for developing significantly deep relationships.

"Impressive." Haley nodded her head. "That's what should be the essence of religion, don't you think?"

"I agree," he said. "So, what church do you attend?"

Haley laughed. "I don't. At least, not at the moment. I'm keeping my options open."

"Wow," she thought. "Here's a guy who knows how to get to the point without a lot of chitchat. I'm going to dig myself into a hole if I don't think up a reason to excuse myself and get back to walking." On the other hand, there was something about Zach's directness that attracted her.

"Do you think it's more important to be honest or to be factual?" he asked.

"Why can't they be the same thing?"

"She's a feisty one, at that," thought Zach.

"They can, but very often there aren't. So, we can spend a lot of time honestly believing something is true when it isn't."

"Well, I suppose that depends on how you define truth, doesn't it?" Haley countered.

It wasn't like Haley was trying to turn the tables on him. She would have taken debate in high school, but figured, what was the use? Haley wasn't going to be a career public speaker, and she hated conflict. But now, from the recesses of her mind, came the desire to clarify and strengthen what conviction she had.

"Can I give an example?"

"Why not?" She said, almost wistfully.

"Say a person believed that a peach tree was an apple tree. That person honestly felt that all the aspects of a peach tree, right down to the fruit, belonged to an apple tree."

"Okay."

"And let's say that same person really, really enjoyed eating what they thought were apples. Even as they were holding the firm fruit, and the warm juice of it spilled over onto their hands as they ate one."

"You're making me hungry!" she said.

"Would that belief turn the peach into an apple?"

"Of course not!" Haley answered.

"So would you agree that, as far as the person was concerned, they thought they were eating an apple?"

"Yes."

"And would you also agree that what they thought was an apple was actually a peach?"

"Sure."

"And that person was honest in their belief?"

"Right, but just because the person was honest about it, that didn't turn the peach into an apple," Haley answered.

Just then, like the proverbial ton of bricks, Haley's disenchantment with Christmas became crystal clear. The true source of her discontent wasn't a lack of justice between the haves and the have-nots, although her own experience when growing up had taught her that. It wasn't the outward trappings of the holiday that had seemed to smother out the rich tradition of saving grace that was made present in the birth of a baby two thousand years ago. It was something else.

"Truth trumps belief then?"

Haley slowly nodded her head.

"You shall know the truth, and the truth shall set you free." Zach spoke out the words from the Gospel of John, Chapter 8.

"That's why Jesus was so insistent about basing our relationship with him on the truth?"

Zach smiled. "Well, he couldn't help it. He was Jewish and he was a rabbi, and he was pretty immersed in a culture that sought after the truth."

"But we can be deceived so easily! No offense, but what about Moses and Egypt? That was forty years of walking around in the desert."

"Even after proof of the truth, we're all capable of turning our backs on it," Zach said.

"Or forgetting it altogether. It's difficult to stay focused on the truth when we're surrounded by so many half-versions of it."

All the Christmas Eves that Haley had spent struggling to make sense of the significance of the season came back to her. The focus on shopping, beginning with Black Friday; the holiday music about mistletoe and fireplaces and snow and Santa Claus and Rudolph. All of it was stripped away now. When she was young, retailers gave a little leeway to celebrate Thanksgiving first. It was its own season. But now, it seemed like the Christmas sales rush began the day after Halloween.

As Haley's brain seemed to be running at a hundred miles an hour, Zach waited for an outward sign that she had reached some sort of conclusion. He found one when she slowly began to smile, wider than she ever had in her life.

"What's happening?" he asked.

"I'm such a judger!" she spat out, almost spontaneously, from a place deep insider her.

"Pardon?"

"I judge people so easily. It's second nature. I'm too lazy to search something out for myself or go beyond my own limited experience. So, I judge because it requires no extra thought. Or I'm so full of fear of something unknown that instead of trying to understand, I judge."

"We all do that."

Haley shook her head. "But I've made it a lifestyle."

She started to shake.

"Are you all right?" Zach asked.

She nodded. "I haven't felt this good in a really long time. I feel like after being stuck inside some sort of emotional prison, God just opened up the door and threw away the keys."

"That was another part of the scripture from Isaiah that Jesus quoted when he was in the synagogue in Capernaum," Zach continued.

"What part?"

"I've come to set the captive free."

It didn't seem possible, but Haley's smile got even wider.

She was willing to let go of the uncertainty ingrained in her as a little girl. She was willing to go beyond her own mother's experience. She was willing to give God a chance and trust someone besides herself. To the average person, it might not have seemed like much, but to Haley, it felt like she had just climbed Mt. Everest and was looking out at the purest blue sky and sunshine.

Freedom!

"That's quite a Christmas present, don't you think?" Zach asked.

"Yes, it is!"

Dan Salerno

Icing on the Cake

There are plenty of stories about successful people who live thousands of miles away from the place where they grew up, but somehow, something happens to bring them back home for the holidays.

Zelda wasn't one of them. She was very successful but had never left Kalamazoo.

Zelda worked for Sarkosy's Bakery part-time. And she had her own catering business. Together, they added up to a good income. The only thing was that sometimes people wanted to get married at the most inconvenient times. Like two days before Christmas.

The reception was going to take place in the space above Just Good Food on Rose Street. The bride and groom were in their 30s and they had saved up money for an intimate and tasteful celebration.

Zelda was providing a menu of pot roast, brown rice, chicken breast in cream sauce, grilled vegetables, and a German chocolate cake to go against the traditional white cake, which neither bride nor groom especially liked.

It was unusually warm the morning of December 23rd as Zelda walked into the building. Her friend Amanda was helping to bring in the trays of food.

"Wow, this is an absolutely gorgeous space!" Amanda said, as they had finished bringing in the last of the food. The tables were covered in white tablecloths. The windows were draped in a sheer ivory-cream linen. The plates were off-white china. The water pitchers were sterling silver, matching the silverware. The glasses were Irish crystal. The floor was black and white squares of ceramic tile. The walls were white oak. Every piece of the décor was elegant yet comfy.

Which was slightly ironic because Amanda had decided years ago that she wasn't the marrying kind. She had been a tomboy growing up, running around with two older brothers, experiencing skinned knees, bruised arms, and injured calves from sliding hard into home plate.

Her teen years were taken up with basketball, track, and cross country. Amanda loved to run. Her feet sailed up the hills on the home cross country course, and her lungs positively reveled in keeping up with her pounding heart as she ran.

But her heart had yet to do flip-flops over a boy.

Zelda, on the other hand, was your classic starry-eyed romantic. The first human emotion she learned to express was sighing. By the time she was one, she had perfected it in all its infinite variations. When she was two years old, she cried uncontrollably while watching a commercial that included a puppy. In between sobbing, she pointed to the screen and said to her mom, "Pup, cute!" And then there was the incident in fourth grade when she verbally lambasted Tommy McVickers on the playground because he rejected her offer of marriage.

"How could you?" she demanded.
"Do what?"
"Not marry me!"
"I'm a kid! So are you!"
"So?"

"Aren't we supposed to date first?"
"What's that got to do with anything? I love you!"
"I don't even know where you live!"

Suffice to say that it ended badly. But that didn't deter Zelda from pursuing despite frequent setbacks. It wasn't as if she was unappealing. She had grown up to be 5'3", with auburn hair that was outrageously curly. She was also feisty and remarkably quick-witted. Maybe it was the luck of the genetic draw. Her father was Jewish, and her mother was Irish. They had met in the 60s at a dance studio in the Milwood neighborhood, and they were a very handsome couple.

It didn't help matters much that Mendel and Shannon Feinstein had a hankering for classic romantic comedies, which they felt were perfectly fine to let Zelda watch along with them. The Feinsteins didn't believe in cable, television news programs, or the earliest versions of reality TV shows, or anything else that would tarnish their perception of the world.

"I wonder what kind of wedding cake Jane Austen would have liked?" Zelda said as she placed the bride and groom figurines on top.

"A chocolate cake with mocha icing in between the layers and dark chocolate icing slathered on top. And on top of it, the statue of the bride would be winning an argument with the groom," Amanda answered.

"Wow."

"She would definitely have used the occasion to make a statement about how silly it was to think anyone could settle down with only one other person for primary social stimulation."

"That's harsh!"
"It's the truth."

Zelda busied herself arranging the bins of food into the steam tables. "It's your opinion, Amanda, born of deep distrust."

"Like Mr. Darcy is going to come to the reception this afternoon and sweep you off your feet?"

"Maybe. You never know."

"This is Kalamazoo, not Netherfield. And did you ever wonder why Jane didn't write a sequel to *Pride and Prejudice*?"

"Because it showed love in its completeness?"

Amanda rolled her eyes. "Because she knew better than to think that Elizabeth Bennet and Mr. Fitzwilliam Darcy could have stayed together for more than a few years, given Elizabeth's brains."

"Being smart isn't necessarily incompatible with having a long-standing relationship."

"If Jane were on the guest list for this event, you could be sure she'd have a thing or three to say about that," Amanda said.

"The bride and groom are in their mid-thirties for crying out loud. They should have enough life experience between them to be spared some of the trials reserved for neophytes."

"Some people never learn from experience, or else they allow that hard-earned perspective to be blurred by love's blindness."

"Love isn't blind."

"It forms emotional cataracts that cloud logic." Amanda seemed determined to resist the romantic atmosphere of the reception space.

By now, they had all the food put up and could rest a moment before moving on to the beverages. Zelda walked over to Amanda, who was standing by the entrance to the serving area, and took her hand. "'I have courted prepossession and ignorance, and driven reason away. Till this moment, I never knew myself.' Does that sound like someone who is allowing love to get in the way of cognitive function?"

Amanda caught the reference to Elizabeth Bennet talking about her own revelation when it came to love. Zelda continued, "To quote Jane, 'Your defect is to hate everybody who could possibly love you.'"

"'And yours,'" Amanda quoted Elizabeth speaking back to Mr. Darcy, "'is to willfully misunderstand them.'"

It was all Zelda could do to shrug her shoulders and point to the cases of bottled water.

"Let's put these guys in the cooler so they'll be ready."

"I'm sorry," Amanda began. "I know I'm coming across as harsh. But it's for your own good."

Before we go any further, you should probably know that Amanda had her own run-in with a boy in grade school. His name was David Wilson but everyone called him Speed for short. He was a boy's boy and was also quite a runner. One sunny, spring afternoon in fifth grade, Speed challenged anyone who was up for it to a race around the school's block.

Amanda had just walked out of the cafeteria into the schoolyard, and when she heard Speed throw down the gauntlet, she walked right up to him.

"I'll do it," she said.

"Do what?" he sneered, standing in the middle of half a dozen of his male friends.

"Race you."

"I don't race girls," he said matter-of-factly.

"What are you afraid of?"

"What part of 'no' don't you understand?"

"I can beat you," she told him.

"I don't like wasting my time."

"You're a coward," Amanda said, turning on her heels to walk away.

At this point, the snicker left Speed's face.

"Hey, wait a minute."

Amanda turned towards him, steely-eyed and determined. She raised her eyebrows, waiting for him to respond.

"Just you and me. After school. Right here."

A smile slowly came to her face.

The rest of the afternoon was a blur to Amanda. She couldn't concentrate on anything except the race. At 3:20 sharp, she walked out the door, and within a minute she was standing exactly on the same spot where she and Speed had their conversation earlier. Speed was already there, standing alone.

"Where's your posse?" she asked.

"I told them to get lost," he told her. "This race is between you and me."

Nevertheless, there was a small group of fifth graders who had heard about the dare and were milling around to watch. Amanda and Speed agreed to count down from 10. They would both shout, "Go," and then head down the street and around the block, returning to the starting point in the playground.

As they began, Amanda saw Speed take off like a rocket ahead of her. She resisted the natural inclination to keep up with him, figuring she wanted to stay strong for the finish, pacing herself. She also figured that Speed was a bit of a show-off, and as soon as he was out of sight of the schoolyard, he would slow down.

When he turned the first corner, he dialed down his pace. Amanda began to catch up. At the second corner, Speed slowed down even more, and by the time they rounded the final corner and headed for home, they were neck and neck.

Heading into the schoolyard, it looked like they were going to collide with each other until Amanda slowly pulled away. She won by a foot.

After she had caught her breath, Amanda went over to Speed, who was hunched over and still winded.

"Nice race," she said, extending her hand.

He ignored her gesture. "Just so you know, I let you win."

Amanda kept her hand out. "You gave it your best shot."

He said nothing and walked away.

In that moment, Amanda decided that boys were too afraid of open competition with girls to bother getting to know each other. If you couldn't be yourself around them, what was the point?

The thing about Amanda was that she hadn't let initial disappointment turn into defeat.

In fact, all things considered, she had gone on from her incident with Speed Wilson to have an outstanding friendship with Rory Martino, who had been watching from the sidelines as Speed turned down her offer of congratulations.

"Boys are not the cleverest organisms on the planet," she muttered under her breath as she walked away from Speed that day.

"You shouldn't go around saying things like that in public," Rory told her as he moved up to walk alongside her. "And would you mind slowing down a bit before we both have heart attacks on school property?"

She kept up her pace but turned to him. "I won't apologize for speaking the truth."

"I didn't ask you to apologize. Just be more careful when you choose to speak it."

"Speed Wilson is a jerk."

"I agree with you."

"And the subset of boys that he represents is way too large."

"Sure, but you're forgetting one slight fact."

"Which is?"

"Boys don't mature at the same rate that girls do. Not to mention the subset that Speed belongs to. It might be to your advantage if you'd cut us some slack. Meanwhile, you can take some comfort from the fact that I'm taking sensitivity training at the Y."

Rory's crack brought a smile to Amanda's face. It was very warm and inviting.

"Who are you?" she laughed.

He took a mock bow. "Rory Martino, at your service."

From that point on, Rory had been her biggest supporter. He was the one she first called up to when she had been admitted to Kalamazoo College. He had been the one to confirm her decision to choose Florence, Italy, for K-College's study abroad program during her junior year. And he had hollered the loudest when she graduated. When she chose a career in marketing, he was thrilled for her. And whenever she faced another disappointment in the romance department, Rory's shoulder was the one she cried on.

Getting back to the Christmas wedding, in no time, Zelda and Amanda had transferred the cases of bottled water into the kitchen cooler.

"Well, the table settings are done, and we've fired up the steam table," Zelda said, glancing at her watch. "All we need to do now is wait."

Amanda laughed. "That's the hardest part, isn't it? I mean, this is a small-scale wedding, but still, we have to deal with the time warp that occurs after the ceremony when all the wedding party photos get taken."

They pulled up a chair in the kitchen and sat down.

"Do you know anyone in the wedding party?" Zelda asked.

"I don't think so. I mean, the bride and groom's families. I am drawing a blank. How about you?"

"Nada." Zelda paused before continuing. "So, what's your own wedding fantasy?"

"Having the groom alive and breathing always helps."

"Come on. I'm serious."

"So am I," cracked Amanda. "It's hard enough communicating with a human, let alone a dead one."

Zelda decided to go for specifics. "So, given a real live *homo sapiens* for your groom of choice, what time of year do you think works best for a wedding?"

"This is going to sound so counterintuitive coming from me, but I actually like December."

"You mean Christmas?"

"I love the snow, and the cold, brisk air, and how moonlight makes the snow sparkle. It's as close to magic as we'll ever get this side of heaven."

"Wow, coming from you, that's an extremely romantic vision."

Amanda raised her eyebrows. "Being a skeptic and having a sense of romance aren't mutually exclusive. It gets us back to Jane Austen and her ability to balance wit with decorum and irony and come out smelling like a rose."

"That's the first thing we've agreed on all afternoon!" Zelda smiled. "We should have had this conversation years ago!"

"Besides, people are more open to being their truest selves this time of year."

Amanda nodded. "It defies reason, doesn't it? There is no denying the powerful effect of peace on earth."

"True confession. You know those Christmas movies you see on the Hallmark Channel? The ones where the main character moves out of town, becomes stressed, and comes back for the holidays to fall in love with someone from their childhood who initially hates them?"

"Sure."

"Even though I'm Jewish, I love them. As long as the production values are halfway decent and the plot is reasonable. Don't tell my rabbi, though."

"Of course."

"I'm joking."

"As long as it's the season, I've always meant to ask, what's with you and Rory?"

"What do you mean?"

"You've known each other since middle school, and you say he's your best friend. It seems like you could take it to the next level."

"No, no, no." Amanda shook her head for emphasis. "That's exactly what Jane's been trying to get across to us. The futility of trying to have it all."

"We aren't living in the eighteenth century like she was," Zelda replied. "Things have loosened up since then."

"I'd rather have an exceptional best friend than a so-so husband. I won't risk it."

"Do you love him?"

"Pardon?"

Zelda put her hand on Amanda's shoulder. "Why do you keep on insisting that friendship ends when love begins?"

"Because I've seen it happen. The minute you bring love into the equation, it spoils everything. Women and men have completely different views of it."

"It doesn't have to be that way."

"You aren't speaking from your own experience, Zelda. You're speaking from your heart, which isn't making sense. The strongest case for what you're saying would be if you had found it in your own life."

"I'm not talking about me. I'm talking about you."

Just then, the side door to the kitchen opened, interrupting their conversation, and in walked Rory.

"Hey!" he said, walking up to Amanda and Zelda as if it were the most natural thing in the world for him to suddenly break into their conversation, giving each of them a hug. "I bet you're surprised to see me!"

"You have no idea," Amanda said.

"We were just talking about..." Zelda didn't get a chance to complete her sentence as Amanda jabbed her sharply in the side.

"The weather," Amanda continued for her. "We were just saying how lovely it is to have a wedding at this time of year."

"It sure is!" Rory was obviously in a very happy mood. "It's Christmas and the season of good cheer, and it's snowing outside to boot. It's great!" He took a closer look at Amanda before continuing. "And you're wondering what I'm doing here, aren't you?"

"Yes, I am."

"Friend of the groom. A friend of a friend, actually. She didn't want to come to the wedding alone, so I'm her date, so to speak."

"Where is she?"

"Outside in the parking lot. Her smartphone rang almost the second we pulled in."

"So!" It was all Amanda could come up with to give herself a few more seconds to ease into a conversation, given her genuine surprise at having Rory show up when he had been the subject of such an intense conversation.

"So," he answered back, his smile still intact. "How's it going, you two?"

"We were just discussing Jane Austen," Zelda piped in. "And her views on..."

Once again, Zelda was the unwilling recipient of a sharp elbow to the side. "...on wedding cake. We were wondering what sort of cake she'd go for."

Rory looked from Amanda to Zelda before answering. "I don't know what Jane felt about cake, but with marriage in general, how about this?

Happiness in marriage is entirely a matter of chance. If the dispositions of the parties are ever so well known to each other or ever so similar beforehand, it does not advance their felicity in the least. They always continue to grow sufficiently unlike afterwards to have their share of vexation; and it is better to know as little as possible of the defects of the person with whom you are to pass your life.

Rory shrugged before going on. "It's from *Pride and Prejudice*. Once an English major, always an English major."

"You see!" Amanda shot Zelda a look. "Dear Jane was a realist at heart!"

Zelda countered, "Then why did she write, 'Oh, Lizzie! do anything rather than marry without affection.'?"

Right then, Amanda was thinking of another, lesser known, work of Jane's, *Northanger Abbey*.

And although Amanda didn't know the words by heart, this is what Jane wrote:

And such is your definition of matrimony and dancing. Taken in that light, certainly their resemblance is not striking; but I think I could place them in such a view. You will allow that in both, man has the advantage of choice, woman only the power of refusal; that in both it is an engagement between man and woman, formed for the advantage of each; and that when once entered into, they belong exclusively to each other till the moment of its dissolution; that it is their duty each to endeavor to give the other no cause for wishing that he or she had bestowed themselves elsewhere, and their best interest to keep their own imaginations from wandering towards the perfections of their neighbors, or fancying that they should have been better off with anyone else.

For a few awkward seconds, Amanda and Zelda stood there, staring at each other. Rory had no idea what had preceded his appearance in the kitchen, but he felt it was his obligation to do what he could to lighten the mood.

"Well, I think Jane summed it up quite nicely by writing, 'Marriage is indeed a maneuvering business.' It's a very complex relationship."

Rory had grown up, gone to Grand Valley State University, and now lived in Grand Rapids. He worked as the communications manager for the Grand Rapids Art Museum (or GRAM for short). Grand Rapids and Kalamazoo were just far enough apart to keep Amanda and Rory from seeing each other on a regular basis.

For his part, Rory remained the same kind-hearted, engaged individual he was as a boy. Even though Amanda's shoulder crying most often happened via late-night phone conversations, the two did meet at least three or four times a year. Alternately in each other's town, depending upon what activity drew them together.

When they did spend time together, Amanda went home with a warm feeling. As if everything was fine with the world. Rory had the same effect on Amanda when on the phone. And whatever event they took part in together, they always enjoyed each other's company.

While Amanda and Zelda's outlook on romance and love seemed to be polar opposites, Rory's view was somewhere in the middle.

"Tell me something," Zelda asked him, point-blank. "Do you believe in marriage?"

"I do. My own parents love each other. I saw it every day growing up, and I still do."

Zelda gave Amanda a look. "At some point, then, you could see yourself getting married? Hypothetically speaking?"

"Of course. Why not?"

"But earlier you said that marriage is a complex relationship," Amanda said, a little surprised.

"Yes, it is. But most things that have substance to them are that way. Even a friendship."

"Like ours?" Amanda was feeling more than a little self-conscious. Although Rory and Zelda knew each other, the three of them hadn't spent all that much time together. What Zelda knew of Rory was primarily through Amanda's eyes.

"Sure." Rory leaned toward Amanda a bit and frowned. "You aren't getting ready to dump me, are you?"

Zelda laughed. "You are her best friend, Rory. I can't tell you how many times she's told me that. She calls you before she calls me about her latest romantic fiasco. That should tell you something."

"That Amanda has me on speed dial and not you?"

"I'm not dumping you," she said, before giving him a playful swat on the arm. "You should know me better than that."

"So, then, what's all this heavy-duty stuff about marriage? I know we're at a reception, but come on, weddings are fun. Receptions are fun. And it's almost Christmas!"

"One of us is feeling a little insecure, that's all," Zelda said.

"It's not insecure to point out how marriage can wreck a totally fine friendship. I've seen it happen. I'm a realist."

"Amanda, that's pretty much the bottom line of all those late-night conversations we've had, isn't it? You're very plugged in to reality, and for you, marriage doesn't fit in that universe."

"Because something like fifty percent of all marriages in the United States end in divorce. It's a recipe for disaster."

"Your brain may be telling you that, but your heart isn't. Why else would you be so disappointed when guys let you down?" he said.

"Just because I'm a realist doesn't mean I like what I'm seeing."

Rory moved in a little closer before continuing. "You've got quite a dilemma going on in there, don't you?"

"Where?"

"In your heart."

Zelda took this as her cue to pull the water bottles out of the cooler and bring them to the serving table in the reception hall, leaving Rory and Amanda alone in the kitchen.

"Don't you, of all people, make fun of me, Rory Martino."

"I'm not making fun, but if your best friend can't point something out to you, who can?"

"Well, this time, I'd prefer if you didn't." The tears slowly started coming down her cheeks. "This really sucks."

"What sucks?"

"I'm losing it in the middle of helping my friend set up for a wedding meal, and I don't have a Kleenex."

Rory reached into his pocket, pulled out a handkerchief, and handed it to Amanda. "You are the patron saint of criers, but I love you anyway."

"What do you mean you love me? You mean as in best friends loving each other?"

By this point, the tears were freely flowing as Amanda blew her nose.

"I mean, I love you. Period."

A few years after Amanda's encounter with Speed Wilson, she walked home from school one day to find her dad lying on the living room couch, with a half-empty bottle of Scotch nearby. It was a week before Christmas, and her parents had been fighting more than usual. Over the past couple days, it had reached a crescendo of allegations yelled at each other. Her dad had the softer personality of the two. It had devastated him to lose his job to downsizing. Amanda's mom, on the other hand, had continued to rise up the corporate ladder.

"Dad!"

When he didn't respond she walked up and shook him. Slowly, he woke up.

"What is it?"

"You've been drinking."

"Sorry, honey. I didn't mean for you to find me like this."

"But I did."

"Yeah. You did. What are you, the family spy? Did your mother put you up to this?"

"I just got home from school, Dad. No one put me up to anything."

"I'm not so sure about that. I don't need another person around here condemning me. I've already got your mom doing a fine job of that."

"I'm not condemning you."

He reached out to slap her, missed, and fell over onto the floor. Shortly afterwards, Amanda's parents were divorced, and she never saw her father again. It was this experience that cemented Amanda's sense of the unreliability of men.

Rory slowly put his hand on Amanda's shoulder, looking her squarely in the eyes.

"I can't help it," she said. "Past experience has hardwired me to question any relationship involving a guy that has the slightest potential for romance."

"So, you can't accept the fact that I love you, no matter what?"

"No, I can't."

"Even though we've been each other's best friend forever?"

"Especially because of that! I just can't do it, Rory."

Rory was silent for a moment. Then he spoke. "I saw a movie once, called *Old Fashioned*. There was a character in that film named Aunt Zella. She was a senior citizen with a lot of wisdom to share with the male lead, named Clay, who was going through a hard time accepting that someone could actually love him."

Amanda attempted to dry her tears. "Aunt Zella?"

He nodded. "So, there's this climatic scene towards the end, and Clay is telling Aunt Zella how unworthy he is. And she looks him in the eye and says, 'Wake up. Get over yourself. You and your pain. Stop using the grace of God as a brick wall. Do you get this upset over children starving? Over anyone else's suffering? ... There's no goodness without mercy. There's no virtue without forgiveness.'"

"Sounds like she was a very wise person."

Zelda walked back into the kitchen just then, catching the tail end of the conversation. "And if she were here right now, she'd be telling you the same thing. It's as plain as the nose on your face that Rory cares for you. And you care for him. You've been best friends since grade school. Isn't that enough of a foundation to go forward, wherever that might be?"

Slowly Amanda nodded her head 'yes.' It was a subtle gesture, but it took a tremendous amount of emotional strength.

Rory thought back to his initial encounter with Amanda, listening to her give the what-for to Speed after that fateful race around the school block. He realized that over the years, his commitment to Amanda had grown. He had been her best encourager and friend, and he would continue to be so.

He gently reached up and wiped a solitary tear off Amanda's cheek, the last remnant of what had been a hailstorm of feelings that cleansed away disappointment and doubt, opening the way for something deeper.

She hugged him close, whispering, "Thank you so very much for your friendship!"

He smiled back. "'Tis the season!"

Dan Salerno

Jersey and the KIA

Jersey walked to her car across the street from the Kalamazoo Institute of Arts (KIA) where she worked part-time, alternating as a receptionist and a cashier in the gift shop.

The week before Christmas was usually slow in terms of visitors to the art galleries, but on the other hand, business picked up in the gift shop as people were searching for that special something.

Jersey's parents named her 38 years ago after one of the Channel Islands, which sit between southern England and France.

During World War II, her grandparents immigrated to the United States after Germany invaded. They never went back. By the time the five-year occupation ended, Bernard and Emma Bartlett had settled in their new homeland quite comfortably. They were on their way to having three children. The youngest, Claire, was rambunctious from the start.

Claire passed that trait along to her twins, Jersey, and her brother, Brelade, named after the Welsh saint. Her husband, Dotsand Russell, added a little bit of stability to the DNA mix, being one hundred percent English.

During their upbringing, Jersey and Brelade had been inseparable. Claire poured into them every bit of knowledge she had gained from her degree at Kalamazoo College (K College), homeschooling them through fifth grade. Dotsand had also attended K College but left in his sophomore year to pursue work as a freelance artist. Kalamazoo was just big enough to support his efforts.

Because of their parents' different experiences with life after college, Jersey had chosen to pursue the academic route, graduating from Olivet College, while Brelade made a comfortable living as a furniture designer, skipping formal academic training for an apprenticeship, eventually settling in Ann Arbor.

Despite Jersey's more traditional approach to gaining experience in preparation for a career, she was nevertheless her mother's daughter. She had carved out a living as a communications manager, specializing in the nonprofit sector. To supplement her income, she worked part-time at the KIA.

Which was why, on December 23, she was in her car, turning north onto Westnedge Avenue, meeting her brother at Shawarma King for lunch.

True to form, Jersey arrived a few minutes before her brother, picking out a booth for them.

"Hey, Sis!" he said, waving as he came into the restaurant.

"Welcome back to West Michigan, brother!" she teased him. He had come in to spend Christmas with his parents, a family tradition.

"How is the Little Apple treating you?" she asked as they both went through the buffet line.

"Work is good. I think I'm actually in a position to take on an apprentice."

Jersey nodded as they sat down. "It's like history coming full circle. It's great that you can mentor someone."

She filled her plate with lentil rice, baba ghanoush, green salad, and shredded beef. "Remember when Mom did her history module on the Civil Rights movement?"

Brelade laughed. "She was a superlative teacher."

"She signed us up to volunteer at the Douglass Community Association doing after-school tutoring. Mom didn't want us to feel out of place with anyone." (The DCA was established by African Americans during WWI to serve African-American soldiers stationed nearby.)

"And we were the only non-Catholic family I knew that had a subscription to *The Catholic Worker* newspaper."

"Have Dad or Mom ever told you if they have a religious affiliation?" Jersey asked.

"I don't remember ever asking them."

To be clear, Claire and Dotsand believed in the Eternal One. But they couldn't seem to settle on a particular denomination. The pattern had been that they would start attending a church, getting involved in any social ministry it provided. Because of their wholehearted commitment, they would soon be very active, but their open-ended interpretation of things didn't always sit well with the leadership. Hence, there was a lot of church movement in the family.

"It was fun being exposed to so many different takes on the gospel, wasn't it?" Jersey said.

Brelade nodded. His mother had gotten into the habit of making extra for supper because she never knew who her husband would bring home to share the meal. He taught art at Kalamazoo Valley Community College, and invitations were spread among faculty and students alike.

Dotsand and Claire firmly believed that the simple act of sharing a meal was essentially a spiritual activity. Who knew what the effects of conversation around the dinner table would have on a student who was struggling with loneliness or a faculty member who would be buoyed by the example of a loving family?

In Dotsand and Claire's home, no political party had a claim on the Almighty.

"Wasn't it nice to grow up not putting God in a box?" Jersey asked.

"Fear of God is the beginning of wisdom," Brelade said, quoting from Proverbs. "The word fear could be translated to mean deep respect or awe."

"Sort of makes us think twice before affixing God's name to anything."

"Heaven help us from assuming we have an inside track to the kingdom."

Jersey laughed. "I miss you."

"Well, Ann Arbor isn't all that far away, you know."

"It's far enough away to keep me from getting in my car to drive there."

"So, bring me up to speed in the romance department. How are things going?" Brelade asked.

Neither Jersey nor Brelade had dated in high school. But they loved to team up with friends to take in movies and concerts or go hiking along the Kal-Haven Trail.

"I'm resigned to my fate," said Jersey.

"What is that supposed to mean?"

"That I no longer look at the weekend as time to do something with that special someone. I'm too old for that nonsense," she answered.

"Isn't that a bit harsh?"

"It's not that at all," Jersey said. "I mean, what does dating accomplish anyway? It may have worked out for you, but for me, it's not a viable option."

"Okay, I lucked out," Brelade said. "I grew up with a sensational next-door neighbor and hung out with her for 18 years, and then we fell in love."

Brelade and Jersey's family had neighbors who were best friends with their parents. And the neighbors had one daughter, Emilee, whom Brelade just mentioned. Both sets of parents referred to their children as The Three Musketeers because they were always together. It didn't hurt that Emilee was bright, funny, and empathetic, with a head of auburn hair that tended to be super-curly in the summer humidity.

In conversations among the three of them, Emilee referred to herself as 'the third twin,' grateful to have grown up with such good friends. It was a pleasant surprise to find that mutual admiration turned into mutual love with Brelade.

"'Lucked out' is not the term I would have used," said Jersey. "You were blessed. Dating is such a bunch of nonsense."

"But, Sis, that's how it works. You grow up; you test people out towards the goal of finding someone who fits."

Jersey rolled her eyes. "Listen to what you're saying. 'Test people out?' If that's the point, then it's no wonder I never had the slightest interest in dating. And you are fortunate that you didn't have to."

"Come on. You know what I mean."

"No, I don't. We were both raised not to follow the crowd, and I'm not about to start doing it now." Jersey rearranged her silverware for emphasis.

"How else are people supposed to get to know each other?" Brelade asked. "It's supposed to be fun."

"Dating sets the stage for a bunch of false expectations that breed false hope. You learn how to be this fake person, and if you fall in love, someone could wind up marrying a false version of you."

"Do you really believe that?"

"Why do you think so many marriages in America wind up in the dumpster?"

"I don't fault dating for that. This isn't 1857. We don't grow up on farms and live our lives within a radius of 20 miles anymore. Options make it more difficult," he said.

"Options may have complicated it a bit, but that's not the main reason."

Brelade put his hands up in a sign of surrender. "Help me understand then."

"We're trained to bail when life becomes inconvenient. You and I, we're the exceptions. Our parents taught us differently."

"So far, I'm with you, Sis."

"Very few of us are encouraged to think for ourselves. If we did, we wouldn't be hooking up and giving away our souls as if it's of no consequence. Do you remember the first essay I ever got published?"

"Sure, I do. You were so excited to get your first check!"

"Remember the subject?"

Brelade nodded. "Spontaneous dating."

"Right. It was a call to cut out the nonsense and find a better way. But I really didn't have an alternative."

"Have you come up with one since?" he asked.

"Sort of."

"I'm all ears."

"For starters, I won't go out with a guy alone. We have to have at least one friend in common who will go with us." Jersey was uncompromising on this principle.

"Go on."

"And there is no second going out without introducing each other to another friend or two."

"Okay. You want someone else's opinion. I get it."

"I'm not wasting time without it. We may have done a lot of church-switching as kids, but I was paying attention to all those youth group teachings."

"Meaning?"

"Meaning I don't date, as in what most people consider dating," Jersey explained. "I have friends who I visit and invite over and socialize with. I have companionship through them. I have a few close friends who I trust, and we tell each other what's going on in our lives. We encourage each other to be better people. But none of it is romantic."

"Isn't that a pretty radical way of handling it?"

"Not when there's so much needless pain and suffering involved. And who set the standard for normal anyway?"

"It's the price you pay for finding true love," Brelade said.

"None of the business of dating has anything to do with finding true love."

"Relax." Brelade held his hands up again. "Trying to lighten the mood. Get you in the Christmas spirit."

"If you weren't my brother, I'd smack you one."

He reached across the table, picking up the pepper shaker. "You know you're my favorite sibling, right?"

She laughed. "I'm your only sib, so what does that say about anything? Except that you stole all the glib genes when you came out of the womb."

"Actually, I think we split them fifty-fifty," he said. "As I recall, you used to be quite the wit."

"I gave being witty up for Lent a few years ago and haven't gotten back into it."

"That's what I'm talking about, Sis!" Brelade held up his hand for a high five. "Don't keep me hanging."

Jersey laughed and high-fived her brother.

"I don't want to get a letter from you one day saying that you've become a nun."

"There are some very, very cool things that nuns are doing nowadays," Jersey shot back. "They're involved in efforts against human trafficking, and they've gone to jail for living out their faith."

Brelade raised his eyebrows. "Jersey, I'm not trying to talk you into getting into the dating game. I know that I was very fortunate with Emilee. She and I had a golden opportunity given to us that most people don't."

"No kidding!"

"It's just that maybe you might consider loosening up your requirements a little."

"Requirements?"

"Most people outside of our family might not share our passion for social justice."

"I wouldn't expect them to, Brelade."

"You know, Dorothy Day talked about the 'long loneliness' of the soul."

"Are you saying I'd be better off hanging out with Catholic Workers again?"

"No, that's not it at all."

"I'm teasing you," she smiled. "Life's short enough as it is. I'm not into adding any unnecessary angst to it."

A week after her graduation from Olivet College, Jersey had moved to Chicago to experience living and working in a Catholic Worker community there. She was involved with the St. Francis House of Hospitality in the Uptown neighborhood. Her time there, working side by side with folks who had very little, cemented her own perspective on what it meant to live by faith. There's something about sharing food that opens up the soul. In fact, Jersey had never quite found an experience to match that time.

"Dorothy would have been the first to admit that communal living in voluntary poverty isn't a bed of roses," said Brelade.

"Yes, but in the same breath she'd be sure to mention that we find our truest selves while serving others."

"Maybe that's what the real dilemma is," said Brelade. "We aren't as inclined to go out of our comfort zone these days."

"We say that life is complicated, and so that complicates our relationships, too, but really, it's not that at all," said Jersey.

"God help us," Brelade said.

Jersey continued, "'Blessed are the meek and the humble of heart, for theirs is the kingdom of heaven.'" She was quoting from the Sermon on the Mount.

Jersey took a good look at her brother. She saw a compassionate, kind, and generous-hearted person. She was proud of him and the work that he did and the life that he and Emilee had built for themselves.

"How's Emilee doing?"

"She's still teaching at the neighborhood elementary school, and she's doing really well, but she had paperwork to catch up on, so she'll be coming into town tomorrow."

"Any plans in the works for little ones?" Jersey asked.

"You know our five-year plan on that."

"I do?"

"Sure. Maybe in another year or two."

"Remember our family's Christmas morning tradition?"

Brelade's grin was wide. "We used to get up early and have eggs Benedict with roasted red potatoes and cherry tarts for dessert."

"Then we would go to church and head out to volunteer at Theo and Stacy's for the community meal downtown," added Jersey.

One of Jersey's most vivid memories of serving Christmas meals was when she was 13. Even with great parents, she was going through a bit of a rough spot as she turned the corner into her teen-aged years. That particular holiday, she was feeling a bit blue because most of the friends she knew were going away on vacation.

It was in this state of mind that Jersey began helping to serve the holiday meal that year, until she came upon a mom with a little girl.

"Would you like turkey or ham?" she asked them.

The child's eyes widened. "You mean we get a choice?" she asked.

"Of course."

"Could I have turkey then, please?"

"Yes. And it comes with mashed potatoes, green bean casserole, and cornbread."

"Mom, we're getting a real meal!"

The mom blushed bright red before talking to Jersey. "I'm sorry, we've sort of been on the road a bit lately."

"On the road?"

"I couldn't make last month's rent, and we've been staying with a friend."

"My mom's friend doesn't have a kitchen." The six-year-old paused. "Or an extra bed, so we sleep on the couch. My name's Becky, by the way."

"Pleased to meet you, Becky. I'm Jersey."

"Honey, I don't think Jersey is interested in our business. She's got a lot of food to bring out." She paused a moment before adding. "Could I please have the ham?"

Becky's face turned into one big frown. "I didn't mean anything by it, Mom."

"It's okay," Jersey said to them. "That's one ham and one turkey!" She started to walk away, but turned back to their table for a moment. "I'm praying that things change for you really soon."

"Thank you," the mom said, offering a hint of a smile. "My name's Lilly."

"After the flower!" said Becky, grinning.

Right then and there, Jersey overcame her teenage angst.

Back at Theo and Stacy's, Brelade stretched out his arms before picking up the conversation. "We really do have incredible parents, don't we? I especially feel it over Christmas, with us being all together."

"We have been blessed, brother," said Jersey, smiling in agreement.

Dan Salerno

Jon and Keisha at St. Bart's

Monday was Jon's day off. He went out for breakfast, then headed uptown to St. Bartholomew's Episcopal Church, a few blocks from Rockefeller Center, where he worked as a news producer at NBC.

Jon soaked in the peace and quiet of the church like he was sunning himself at Jones Beach. He could feel it calm him as he closed his eyes, the sanctuary's grace being shared with some homeless folks who had come in out of the cold.

After a few minutes, the main altar caught his attention, and he found himself thrown back to his middle school days when he became an altar boy. He remembered cutting through Central Park in the summer months on Sunday mornings on his way to serve Mass.

His parents had an apartment crosstown on Columbus Avenue, but they loved the social commitment of St. Bart's, so they had chosen it as their place of worship. All things being equal, it wasn't the liturgy that captured Jon's interest as much as the parish's decision to view themselves as stewards of God's resources, which naturally included treating others as equals.

Those Sunday morning walks through the park were just as formative for him as any sermon. Jon remembered several conversations he had with "street folks." When he was 10 years old, he asked his parents if he could make some sandwiches and hand them out. They agreed and went with him, normally sticking to a section of the park near the 72nd Street entrance across from Central Park West.

The unhoused women and men gradually came to know Jon and engaged him in conversation. Most of them were unfailingly polite and genuinely thankful for the simple gesture of being treated like a human being.

Of course, there was always the occasional conversation that took a bizarre turn.

"What kind of remuneration is this?" asked a man with snow white hair and a beard that was long and frazzled, making him look like a Santa Claus struck by electricity.

"What do you mean?" a young Jon had asked.

"You know exactly what I'm talking about!" the man answered, lowering his eyes. "'There is a basin in the mind where words float around on thought and thought on sound and sight. Then there is a depth of thought untouched by words, and deeper still a gulf of formless feelings untouched by thought.'"

(At the time, Jon was way too young to realize the man was quoting from *Their Eyes Were Watching God*.)

"I'm not sure what you're talking about," was all he could say, even smiling when he said it.

The man continued. "'They sat in company with the others in other shanties, their eyes straining against crude walls and their souls asking if He meant to measure their puny might against His. They seemed to be staring at the dark, but their eyes were watching God.'"

Jon had no way of knowing who Zora Neale Hurston was or anything that she had written. He simply continued to respond in the best way he knew how, with respect for this well-worn individual and for all that he had been through.

For his part, the man kept up his stream of consciousness. "'Death is not an adventure to those who stand face to face with it.'" He nodded staring Jon right in the eyes, as if to dare him towards a rebuttal.

"Pardon?"

"It's from the introduction to *All Quiet on the Western Front*."

"I've never read it."

"You strike me as a boy who would appreciate Remarque. Shall I continue?"

Jon only nodded, transfixed.

"'I see how people are set against one another, and in silence, unknowingly, foolishly, obediently, and innocently slay one another.'"

"Why do you feel this way?" Jon said, asking the question not from an understanding of the subject matter, but rather, out of sheer empathy for the distraught look that was etched on the man's face.

"Jesus said there would be wars and rumors of wars. He must have been thinking of Ecclesiastes. 'Everything is meaningless, completely meaningless!'"

Luckily for Jon, his Sunday school class had been right in the middle of studying that very book of the Bible. In fact, over the course of three weeks they had memorized the first eight verses of Chapter 3, so he quoted them easily:

To everything there is a season,
A time for every purpose under heaven...

With that, Jon handed the man a sandwich. The man slowly unwrapped it, looked up at him, and smiled.

"You seem to have an affinity for the afflicted," the man said.

"I'm not sure what you mean," Jon said.

The man smiled. "I mean you have a natural desire to reach out to others because you care about them. It's a very rare quality."

"It's only a little bit of food," he replied.

"To you, that may be perfectly true, but to me, it's better than a Thanksgiving dinner."

"Really?" Jon's eyes had gotten wider with the anticipation of getting to know this very interesting person who seemed to know so much but had so little.

"'Blessed is the person who considers the poor,'" he said, quoting from Psalm 41. 'That person will be blessed on the earth.' Do you know what that means?"

"Not exactly," Jon answered.

"God has a special concern for the least of us. In fact, God loves the least of us so much that there's a special blessing for those who help ensure that we're not forgotten."

"Really?"

"'God raises the poor out of the dust and lifts the needy out of the ash heap; That God may seat them with princes – with the princes of God's people.'" The man's eyes were positively twinkling. "Psalm 114. You can check it out for yourself sometime. Poor or rich. With or without. In God's eyes, we're all the same. We on earth tend to forget that."

The man took a bite of his sandwich before continuing. "The Bible contains more references to the poor and how they should be treated than on most any other subject. So why is it that there are so many people who have so little in the middle of a city that has so much?"

"I don't know." Jon shrugged his shoulders.

"In my case it was Vietnam. But it could have been most anything. All's I know is, I began drinking when I got back home from the war to chase the devil away, and I wound up replacing one nightmare with another."

"But you don't seem to be drunk now," Jon had said, being the sort of person who was used to taking things at face value.

"Young man, had we met later in the day, I'm quite sure I would have been quite incapable of chatting with you at all."

"No kidding!"

"Unfortunately, I'm not. May I ask you another question?"

"Sure," Jon nodded.

"Why do you spend time handing out food to strangers?"

"It's sort of complicated, actually."

The man laughed again. "How so?"

"I began doing this because I learned that it's a good thing to help other people. Just like you said."

"Go on," the man encouraged Jon to continue.

"I'm not going to let how the rest of the world treats the poor stop me from doing something about it."

"Good for you, young man!" the man said. "I commend you for your heart towards others."

"Commend?"

"Salute. Recognize. Appreciate. Praise."

Now it was Jon who was smiling. "Thank you!"

"No thanks necessary, young man. God sees what you're doing, and God loves it. There's actually a reward waiting for you in Heaven for what you're doing on earth today."

Jon was positively intrigued. "Really?"

"Absolutely. The Jews call it a mitzvah. God's growing your heart. That's actually the biggest part of your reward. And the mystery of it. What you're doing today. This very conversation. All of it's connected. And it pleases God."

Jon's mind slowly brought him back to St. Bart's.

It wasn't just another Monday off from work. It was a few days before Christmas. He had shopping to do and was just about to get up when someone began playing the organ. The tone was rich and deep, and Jon recognized the tune. It was Handel's Messiah and a singer up in the choir loft began practicing the opening from Isaiah 40:1-5.

Comfort, comfort my people, says your God.
Speak tenderly to Jerusalem.

*Tell her that her sad days are gone
and her sins are pardoned...*

*Fill in the valleys
and level the mountains and hills.
Straighten the curves,
and smooth out the rough places.
Then the glory of the Lord will be revealed...*

Fifteen years after having the conversation with the man in Central Park, Jon seldom stopped when walking through the same park anymore. He had places to go. People to meet. It seemed like his life was one long series of engagements that didn't go much further than the surface.

What happened? Why hadn't he noticed the road that he was headed down?

The singer began again, this time from Isaiah 60:1-3:

*Arise, Jerusalem! Let your light shine for all to see.
For the glory of the Lord rises to shine on you.
Darkness as black as night covers all the nations of
 the earth,
but the glory of the Lord rises and appears over you.*

All nations will come to your light...

It wasn't as if his job at NBC was boring. He had been promoted several times and was now on track to get the executive producer's job when she retired at the end of the year. That's it, he figured. Just a case of the nerves. Of course, he'd go from working 40 hours a week to 60. But it was worth it because he'd finally have a say in what actually went on the air. Keeping your nose to the grindstone paid off.

The singer continued once again from Isaiah 9:1-2 this time:

*The people who walk in darkness will see a great light.
For those who live in a land of deep darkness,
a light will shine.*

It seemed as if Jon's spirit was moving along with the music, influencing his thoughts. Something inside him that had been dormant was beginning to spring to life, as if responding to the very words from scripture that Handel had chosen for his composition.

The ethereal became crystal clear as the singer finished up from Isaiah 9:6:

For a child is born to us
a son is given to us.
The government will rest on his shoulders.
And he will be called:
Wonderful Counselor, Mighty God,
Everlasting Father, Prince of Peace.

Jon sat for a moment, closing his eyes, soaking in the last remaining echoes of the pipe organ's magnificence. Then he slowly got up, spotting a seemingly unhoused woman who was sitting in a pew towards the very back of the church. She smiled as he got closer, and something inside him decided to return the gesture.

"Hello," he began.

"It's a difficult thing to be in the presence of a holy God," she whispered.

Jon wasn't sure where this conversation was going, but he was no longer in any kind of a hurry.

"I suppose."

"That's why I sit back here, so I can see most of the sanctuary and stay in awe."

Jon just arched his eyebrows, inviting the woman to go deeper.

"I wasn't always like this. Used to have a seat in the second row, to the right. My family came here faithfully every Sunday. You could say we were sitting in the gold seats."

"So, what happened, if you don't mind me asking?" Jon asked.

"My appetite for this world got too big, and it ate the soul right out from under me."

She stared at him before proceeding. "I grew up in church but grew out of it during college. Classic case of a thinking person's response to organized religion."

"How so?"

"Between scholarships and my parent's money, I could afford Harvard, so I went there and got a so-called education. Nothing against the Ivy League, but they'd be better off remembering why their schools were started in the first place."

(Jon guessed she was referring to John Harvard's desire to help establish a college to train preachers. Many other Ivy League schools had similar histories.)

"A bit of an abandonment of veritas, eh?"

She smiled at the reference. "You'd have to recognize something in order to abandon it." She paused a moment, giving Jon a chance to take his own second look. He guessed she was his age, give or take a couple of years. And her eyes were remarkably clear. Her apparel, while plain, was clean. It was then that he realized she probably wasn't homeless at all. "You strike me as being one who's abandoned something."

He swallowed hard before answering. "I didn't realize it until a few minutes ago." He felt like introducing himself to make the conversation more personal, extending his hand to her. "My name's Jon."

She took his hand. "Keisha. Pleased to meet you." She smiled again. Her teeth were perfect; in fact, they were beautiful. "So, now that we've got the pleasantries completed, how about answering the question?"

"*A sharp one,*" Jon thought. "I was sitting up there, closer to the altar, and out of nowhere I remembered a homeless guy I met years ago."

"Out of nowhere?"

"Years ago, I used to hand out food in the park. And one day, a man and I had a great conversation."

"He must have made an impression on you."

"I didn't realize it at the time, but he was trying to help me figure out what to do with my life."

Keisha moved over, motioning for Jon to sit down before asking, "And did you?"

He accepted her invitation and continued. "I like what I'm doing, and I make good money. I'm in line for a major advancement, and I'll be in a position to change things."

Jon noticed that Keisha smelled like ivory soap and lavender. He realized that if she was wearing older clothes, it wasn't because she had to.

"So, let me turn the tables and ask you something," he said. "You've mentioned you had a great education and that you used to sit up front in this church. I'm curious, what happened? Are you a third-generation hippie?"

Keisha laughed and caught herself. "Sorry, if we weren't in St. Bart's, it wouldn't matter. But they are very gracious about opening up their doors, and I don't want to wreck it for the folks who have no place else to go." She cleared her throat before continuing. "My dad was a lawyer for the ACLU, and my mom is a senior editor at HarperCollins. We grew up with a very progressive point of view in our home."

"No kidding! So why didn't I run into you when I was handing out sandwiches in the park?"

"My activism didn't kick in until college. After I graduated, I got a job with the Community Service Society. Then my father passed away and left an inheritance. So I didn't have to work if I didn't want to."

Jon gave out a low whistle. "Must be nice!"

"It is. But I have also been saving my own money for a decade. Anyway, the important thing wasn't the money."

"It's not?"

"Absolutely not. It's the time it buys you. For six months, I've been coming here every Monday to pay my respects."

In response to the frown on Jon's face, she continued. "I mean, the Bible says that fear of the Lord is the beginning of wisdom, right?"

"Sure."

"That word 'wisdom' can be translated as 'intimacy' or 'deep understanding.' So that's what I've been doing. Getting to know God better. I realize what a windfall I've gotten having financial security. But that's only part of it. I need wisdom in figuring out what to do next."

Keisha had gone to church with her family growing up, but her parents had treated it as a social event rather than anything spiritual. They believed in God but were perfectly comfortable believing from a distance. College had only reinforced this behavior. But recently, Keisha had consistently given serious thought to going beyond the Sunday morning requirement.

"I come here every Monday morning," Jon confessed. "But it's not to get closer to God. I need the peace and quiet, and probably on some subconscious level, my spirit is tapping into eternity here."

"I think it's providential. You come here every Monday. So do I, but usually it's later in the afternoon. But for some reason, this morning, something told me to get here earlier. There was an itch."

"An itch?" Jon asked.

"An itch in my spirit. In the past, I would have ignored it, and our paths would never have crossed. But lately, I've come to realize that God really does work in mysterious ways."

"How so?"

"If you believe that God controls the universe because God made it, then is it such a stretch to believe that God can arrange moments in time?"

"That sounds logical."

"It does, except God isn't under the same constrictions as human logic."

Jon was beginning to sense that his spirit was being nudged. In the past he would have been oblivious to it, but not today, not this morning, not with Keisha.

"So does the spirit overrule the mind?"

She shook her head. "As near as I can tell, God brings all the parts of our being together. It's the only way that we become whole."

Jon sighed before continuing. "Well, it would be just like God to have this conversation with you happen right when I was up for a major promotion."

Keisha laughed. "The bonds of practicality, eh?"

"I've worked very hard to get to this point. And I am very close to being on the fast track towards the top."

"It's really none of my business, but you aren't really talking as if this promotion is much more than a salary advance."

"I get to provide creative input and influence programming," he said in his defense.

"Sounds like you're trying to define who you are by what you do for a living."

"What's wrong with that?"

"I think there was a reason that you were in this church today, thinking of the homeless man you once knew."

"It was a nice memory. I'll give you that. But truthfully, things change as you grow up. Even the Bible talks about putting the things of childhood behind."

"When Paul wrote that, he was describing spiritual maturity, not avoidance."

"I have to make a living."

"No argument there."

"I have to look out for myself."

"Even at the expense of putting others behind?"

"No offense, but most of us don't have an inheritance to buffer real life."

Keisha took a deep breath before responding. "No, we don't. But you don't know how I've used mine."

Jon instantly realized how great a judgment he had placed on her. "You're absolutely right. I haven't."

"With some help, I set up a nonprofit that provides college scholarships for low-income kids who show potential. I help fund it through a few small businesses that rent office space."

"You own a building?"

"I own it in partnership with the tenants."

While in college, Keisha had chosen to minor in business administration. Admittedly, the combination of social work and business seemed weird, on the surface. At first, she wasn't exactly sure what had possessed her to pursue such divergent subjects.

"I'm sorry. The truth is, I'm as selfish as they come. You challenge and sort of frighten me at the same time."

In an instant, Keisha went from being mildly annoyed to being empathetic. "Why would I frighten you? We're sitting here in one of the safest, most inviting places in Manhattan."

"That's just it."

She was genuinely puzzled at his response.

Jon continued: "I come here because I feel perfectly safe. Safe to keep on approaching God as long as God doesn't ask me to get outside of my comfort zone. But today I happened to strike up a casual conversation with a total stranger who is challenging me."

Keisha laughed. "All I'm doing is nudging you a little bit."

"But it feels like more than nudging."

"Then maybe you should ask where those feelings are coming from?" She paused for a moment. "Who is doing the challenging if it isn't me?"

Jon thought for a moment before answering. "The same person who is about to ask you if you'd like to continue this conversation over lunch."

Keisha smiled. "Do you feel obligated to feed every stranger who crosses your path?"

He laughed. "Call it an early Christmas present."

Dan Salerno

Kristie's Red Potato Skillet

Kristie wasn't the sort of person who needed an alarm clock to wake up. Usually, she was out of bed by 5 to work the morning shift as a waitress at Roxie's. It didn't hurt that her cat, Buddy, a long-haired black-and-white who was 90 percent tail, jumped on her bed as a backup.

She loved everything about the breakfast shift: the smell of coffee being made; the easy banter with the head cook, SueAnn, as she prepared a batch of scrambled eggs; helping out during the rush by making the orders of toast; the hiss of the hash browns being turned over on the grill.

She loved all the behind-the-scenes magic, but it was her customers who made her day. From the very first person who walked through the door at 6 AM (usually on their way to work) to the senior citizens, most of whom arrived a good two hours or more later. She especially liked them because their easy-going affability matched her own.

Each customer received a genuine smile, slow and a bit shy.

On this particular Monday morning, Kristie was especially excited as she spoke with SueAnn.

"I think I've got a new special for us!"

SueAnn leaned against the cooler door, raising her eyebrows. She had worked with Kristie long enough to know that her specials were always a hit with customers.

"It's a red potato base with scrambled eggs topped with a modified hollandaise sauce."

"And?"

SueAnn knew the way that Kristie's brain worked, and there had to be a combination of spices that would be guaranteed to elevate any ingredient to mouth-watering status.

"I added curry powder to the eggs and a light dusting of tarragon to the potatoes after pan-frying them in olive oil. And I used a bit of Kerrygold Dubliner cheese in the hollandaise to mix it up a bit."

"Wow!"

"Yeah, I know!" Kristie smiled. "Brilliant, right?"

Kristie wasn't one to brag; it was only that her culinary creativity expressed itself with an outward enthusiasm that was as genuine as her smile. The fact that it was two days before Christmas, her all-time favorite holiday, only added to the excitement she was feeling.

"Cook some up after we close out lunch, and if the servers like it, you've got tomorrow's special."

It went without saying that Kristie had brought the spices and Kerrygold with her. "Thanks, SueAnn," she said. "I bow to your gracious nature. We're going to have the best Christmas Eve ever!"

Which was saying a lot because Roxie's, being on Gull Road, was a major East-West artery leading into Kalamazoo. It was also a stone's throw from Borgess Hospital, with hundreds of employees eager to escape cafeteria cooking, if only for some fresh air during their shift.

Christmas Eve dawned with the promise of the infant savior as well as a brand-new entree for the day.

"I'm super excited today, Buddy!" she said, getting out of bed and stroking her cat behind his ears, eliciting an instant purr the size of a diesel engine.

Once at work, Kristie only took a second to think of naming it before writing her creation down on the menu board in bright yellow and green: Red Potato Skillet.

When she finished putting up the menu board, Margie, the manager, shook her head.

"What's wrong?"

"Put your name on it," Margie responded. "I had some yesterday, remember? It's delicious, and it's got your signature all over it."

As Kristie made the edit and finished setting up her station, she couldn't help but anticipate how her Skillet would go over with the early morning crowd.

Before nine o'clock, 15 regular customers had ordered it, and without exception, the compliments came flying into the kitchen by way of the servers.

An hour later, most of the regular breakfast crowd were finishing up when a short, balding senior guy came through the lobby, pausing by the "PLEASE WAIT TO BE SEATED" sign.

In less than a minute, the greeter led him to a booth, where he sat down and began to read over the menu.

Kristie walked over to him. "Coffee?"

"Decaf and a glass of water, please."

She smiled and brought back the coffee and water. "Would you be interested in hearing what our specials are today?"

He looked up at Kristie and nodded.

"We've got pecan waffles, blueberry pancakes, corned beef hash made with leftover pot roast from last night, and Red Potato Skillet."

At the mention of the last option, Kristie saw the man's eyes light up. "What's that last one?"

"It's a bed of red potatoes topped with scrambled eggs with curry powder, hollandaise sauce on top, with Kerrygold Dubliner cheese added to it," she said enthusiastically. When he frowned at the mention of the final ingredient, she added, "It's like Swiss, only nuttier, and it's amazingly creamy because it comes from Ireland."

"That sounds delicious," he said. "But why is it called Kristie's Skillet?" He had noticed the name on the menu board.

"Well, I happened to create it," she said, turning beet red. "And that's my name."

For a 32-year-old with thick, wavy red hair and sky-blue eyes, Kristie wasn't one to fulfill the stereotype of her hair color, at least not with someone she didn't know. For the most part, she channeled her feistiness into the kitchen.

The man smiled. "That settles it then. I'll have some."

A few minutes later, Kristie was back at his booth with a generous portion of her breakfast entrée. For some reason, she felt like engaging him in conversation beyond the normal banter, and because business had slowed down, she began: "I don't think you've come to Roxie's before, have you?"

He shook his head. "I live downtown, on South Street."

Not noticing a ring of any kind on his hands, she offered. "I love that street! Lots of old, elegant, big homes there."

"That's true, but I live in a condo, a block away from the Institute of Arts."

"Must be nice living downtown, so convenient to everything."

Kristie had grown up on Chicago Avenue, off East Main Street. In the 1950s, it had been a solid, working-class neighborhood. By the time her mother had sent her five-year-old daughter to live with her grandparents, turning legal custody over to them, the area was already in decline. The home was kept in good repair, but it was fighting a losing battle as more and more residents got older, retired, and moved out or passed away.

Which is what eventually happened to her grandparents. They died within two years of each other, when Kristie was in her 20s. She was given the house mainly because her mom had been an only child, and she had moved out of state years before, choosing not to stay in communication with her parents.

She had asked her grandparents several times why her mom had made the choice to leave. "Sometimes life doesn't work out like we'd like it to, honey," her grandmother had told her. "And sometimes when that happens, it's best not to spend a lot of time trying to figure out why."

"Living downtown has its advantages," he said. "I like the energy of the city, and it helps with the work I do. The name's Lyle, by the way."

Lyle had worked for the city, handling communications for them. A few years before, he was offered a severance package as part of a downsizing scheme, and he gladly took it. Having a few years yet to go before retirement, he had chosen to set up his own public relations firm. He really didn't need the money, but he wasn't ready to quit working altogether.

Kristie could tell, just from the upscale clothes that Lyle was wearing, that he was fairly well off. He had a silk shirt and tailored suit that was bought in Chicago, all accentuated by a $75 tie. And the fact that he was eating his first meal of the day at the off-hour of 10:30 AM, meant he set his own timetable.

Lyle's financial advisor had invested his money wisely, and he was living on the fruit of it. What Kristie didn't know was the emotional weight that he was carrying after his divorce. It had been 15 years, and the scar tissue formed around his heart had prevented him from engaging anyone on a very deep level. He had gotten so good at dodging intimacy that it was like second nature to him.

On the other hand, Kristie was living proof that a person didn't need to be defined by their past. The love she had received from her grandparents more than compensated for the lack of a mother or father. There are some people who embrace who they are without reservation, choosing to look beyond the present towards the eternal, and Kristie was one of them. She was an old soul with a heart as young as the sunrise.

"What sort of work do you do?" she asked.

Lyle instinctively arched his eyebrows like he always did before giving a smart-alecky answer. "You could say I'm a professional liar."

"Pardon?"

"I used to be the director of communications for the city."

Kristie whistled softly. "Wow. I bet you were really, really good at it."

Lyle let out a laugh. He was a reserved person, but he had a very deep sense of humor. "At lying? I must have been. They kept me around for 28 years."

"I didn't mean it that way," she said, trying to backtrack. "I only meant that you strike me as being a person who's self-assured."

She felt as if the restaurant had switched to an alternate time zone where everything was going in slow motion. By this point, all the other customers had cleared out of her station. Kristie was not one to invest minutes in idling, but for some unknown reason she found herself putting her coffee pot aside and sitting down across from Lyle.

"Sometimes self-assurance is like a lake in the wintertime, when the water is frozen just enough below the surface. You learn how to live by skimming along the top without risking breaking through the ice."

For his part, Lyle didn't know why he was opening up like this. He wasn't one to explore his emotions. As far as gaining any understanding of the relationship between emotional intimacy and relationships, his career choice ironically didn't transfer over into his personal life.

"Walking on lakes in the wintertime is one of my favorite things to do!" she shot back. Every February, when everyone else was complaining about the cold weather, Kristie had taken the bus to Woods Lake and ventured out. She was continually amazed at how it felt to be only a few yards from shore, standing on something that normally wasn't solid.

Speaking of which, one of her favorite childhood memories was of attending the Church of God off East Main Street, the day the youth pastor talked about Jesus walking on water. When the pastor had asked the class, "Does anyone know what that must have felt like?" Kristie excitedly raised her hand and said, with determination, "Yes, I do!"

"So, you've had some experience with that, I take it?" Lyle asked, point-blank.

"Oh, yeah! Plenty! You know how most people want to go to the beach in the summertime when it's good and hot? I was just the opposite. I waited until the middle of wintertime. I mean, what's the adventure in going swimming in the lake when you can wait and walk on it?"

"You weren't afraid?"

She shook her head.

"But didn't your parents pull you back? I mean, they couldn't have approved."

She shook her head again. "I grew up with my grandparents, and I told them I was going downtown with my friends to the movies."

Lyle took a closer look at Kristie and saw the determination in her chin. "But at least you didn't go alone."

Kristie let out a laugh. She was thoroughly enjoying talking to this senior citizen. "Actually, most of the time I did. Didn't you ever go off and do something like that when you were a kid?"

"My father was a business owner, and my mother taught third grade. They were planners, and I wasn't exactly encouraged to be spontaneous."

"Neither was I, but it's like grass that shoots up and grows through the cracks in concrete. What are you going to do? It's there."

He smiled. "I suppose it is. But you're young. You have your whole life ahead of you. You have more time to take the road less traveled."

"That's not true." She was adamant. There were times that Kristie had wanted to take her grandparents by the hand and get them on the bus to take them out of their neighborhood and their comfort zone. Even before she had come to live with them, they had fallen into a routine. Having a granddaughter to take care of had only made them more security-conscious. And although Kristie appreciated the foundation her grandparents had provided, she hadn't let it define her.

"We're all creatures of habit," Lyle said, not sure if he still believed it.

Kristie sat up and looked him straight in the eye. "Don't you think that sometimes we use that as an excuse to stay trapped in habitual ways of living?"

"Unfortunately, a lot of life is like that." This young woman was challenging him, and to his surprise, Lyle was finding that he liked it.

"I don't mean to pry, but if your clothes are any indication, you don't seem to have any financial worries that would constrict your way of living."

She was also bringing out the smarty-pants in him. "Maybe I know a really good consignment shop."

"What you're wearing is too new. I hope you don't take this the wrong way, but you really don't have much practice at debating, do you?"

He shrugged. "You have to like social interaction to debate well."

Lyle had two older brothers, but they were significantly older than he was. By the time he was born, one was a senior in high school, and the other was already in college. They had no interest in developing a bond with a little baby. And his parents had enough on their hands dealing with a surprise child.

Thus, from the time Lyle could walk, he was unconsciously aware that he needed to be a productive member of his family – he was potty trained and learned to eat on his own in record time – and he got his first job, helping his next-door neighbor, who ran a CSA, when he was seven. During the growing season, the neighbor took Lyle with him to the Bank Street Farmer's Market to help him sell his produce. Having a kid there gave him an edge over the other farmers.

The farmer's market stint was important for Lyle because it got him into the habit of interacting with others at an early age. He saw his neighbor engage in the usual customer banter, but Lyle quickly learned that he didn't have the gift of making small talk.

From his earliest days in school, he had excelled in grammar. It was logical, controlled, and didn't require much human interaction. Although his parents insisted that he go to college, it was purely Lyle's decision to focus on writing, which eventually led to his position with the city. As long as he could control the situation, he was totally comfortable writing press releases, overseeing the social media accounts, and even bantering with reporters.

"But you were in the communication business!" Kristie pointed out.

"Yes, with emphasis on the business. I knew how to control the message."

"Are you controlling it now?" She arched her eyebrows for emphasis.

"What do you mean?"

"This isn't a common occurrence for you, is it?"

"Pardon?" What was she getting at, he wondered? When he had walked into Roxie's, he was looking for breakfast, not a conversation. That's why his favorite partner at a meal eaten out was usually a good book.

"Making conversation," she said. "You strike me as the kind of person who could very well go for a week without talking with anyone outside of work."

If Kristie spent more than a few hours without talking with someone, she'd burst. It wasn't that she was a compulsive talker. It was more like she was so genuinely interested in people that she couldn't help interacting with them. She got her energy, her joy, and her fulfillment from the people around her.

"I didn't have the advantage of growing up in a very sociable household," he offered.

"Me, either. But I didn't let my home experience limit me."

Lyle held up his hands in mock self-defense. "I seem to sense a pattern here."

Kristie laughed. "What are you doing on Christmas Eve?" she asked.

"Nothing extraordinary."

"Then why don't you come to my church? We're having a special candlelight service with carols and a kids' program. I'll meet you in the lobby, so you won't be alone."

Lyle was taken aback. Truth be told, he had never stepped inside a church in his life. His family hadn't been particularly religious. Neither was he.

"Well, I don't know."

"What's to know? I'm not asking you to convert. I'm only extending an opportunity for adventure." Kristie couldn't help smiling.

"What's so funny?"

"You are. I mean, I'm giving you the perfect chance to meet some amazing people, and some of them happen to be women and maybe one of them might find you interesting."

"I don't need a partner."

"Of course you do. How else are you going to break out of your shell? I don't mean to be rude, but you aren't exactly a spring chicken. Relatively speaking, the clock is ticking, you know?"

This time it was Lyle who couldn't contain his smile. As a matter of fact, he burst out laughing.

"So, you find my generous invitation amusing?"

"Well, I do, in a way. But that's not what I find funny."

"Is it my pillow hair? I didn't have a chance to wash it this morning. Sort of looks like I slept with my head in a box, doesn't it?"

"You don't have funny hair. It suits you just fine."

"Then what is it?"

"You're sort of daring me to come to your church, aren't you?"

"I'm appealing to your inner sense of adventure. You haven't had one in a long time, and it's high time you did."

"And you also think relationships solve everything."

"No, I don't," she whispered for emphasis, "but I have the intuitive feeling that in your case, it definitely couldn't hurt."

"How do you know that?"

"We all need relationships. I relate to the restaurant manager here and the head cook. Because I relate to them, they let me try out the breakfast special that you ate today. Which you seemed to enjoy, judging from your empty plate."

"Yes, it was delicious. But from my end, it was purely a business transaction. I was hungry, and you offered a very appealing option."

"But it wasn't purely business, or we wouldn't be here talking, would we?"

Kristie figured a guy like Lyle didn't stick around restaurants making small talk. She was savvy enough to realize that her moment of opportunity was here, and she was doing her best to seize it. She knew he had business smarts. But she also knew she had people smarts, which in normal circumstances would triumph.

For his part, Lyle was thinking it had been a long time since anyone piqued his interest like Kristie. In a matter of a few minutes, she had moved from being a waitress to being the creator of an amazing breakfast entrée to being a social secretary, and she was fast becoming a friend.

"You certainly have a way of putting things."

Kristie smiled and stretched before responding. "Someone once told me I have a gift for overstating the obvious. I don't mean to bore you to tears. I'm just responding to what I'm seeing."

And what she saw was a senior citizen in need of a friend.

"You aren't boring me. I would have to say that it would be highly unlikely that you could bore anyone, unless they were comatose."

"So how about it? It's Christmas Eve. Come to the service tonight. Meet me inside the church lobby at 6:30." She pulled the pencil and meal ticket from her pocket, wrote down the address, and handed it to him. "If I don't introduce you to at least three eligible, age-appropriate women, you can come back here for breakfast, and it's on me."

He had a huge, ear-to-ear grin on his face now. It was the first time he felt genuinely at ease with someone in years. In fact, it was longer than he could remember. He could feel himself relaxing as he continued the conversation. "You're serious, then?"

"About meeting a few potential female friends?"

Lyle shook his head. "If you're serious about the free breakfast guarantee that goes along with it, the answer is yes."

Kristie slowly smiled, looked Lyle in the eye, and laughed.

Lunch Lady

"**M**erry Christmas, Mrs. Shevlin!"

Ever since the beginning of December, the kids in the lunch line at Cristo Ray High School on E. 106th Street had been greeting Sophie the same way. They were oblivious to her responding, "And a Happy Hanukkah to you too!"

"What are they teaching these no-thinks anyway?" she couldn't help pondering. "Don't they understand that their Messiah was Jewish?"

It wasn't a train of thought fueled by belligerence as much as an active expression of her practicality. Which was well suited for running a school cafeteria that was exceptional. So much so that some of the kids had taken to walking through the cafeteria at the end of the school day so they could pick up take-out boxes to bring home any leftovers.

One of those kids was Misty Bertolli. She was one of the sweetest, kindest high school seniors you'd ever want to meet. But Misty got a bit overly excited when trying to explain the concept of transubstantiation to Mrs. Shevlin.

"It's literally taking the bread as being Christ's body and the wine as being Christ's blood," she said.

"Sweetheart, that doesn't sound appealing," said Mrs. Shevlin.

"I could see where you'd think that, but it's not, because the wine and bread don't actually change form until the priest says so."

"Father Hoover does this?"

"Well, yeah. During the Mass, at the consecration."

"That's the part when the altar kids ring the bells, right?"

"Of course."

"What do you mean 'of course'? I went to synagogues, not churches." Mrs. Shevlin wasn't being mean; she was only stating a fact in the best way she knew how.

Misty felt the need to apologize. Among all the students at Cristo Rey, she was one of the few who understood Mrs. Shevlin's reference to Hanukkah.

"I'm sorry, Mrs. Shevlin. I didn't mean any offense. Sometimes I get a little carried away."

Mrs. Shevlin smiled before responding, "Misty, totally understandable," and giving her a double portion of the meatloaf.

On Saturdays, Misty led a group of interdenominational youth who volunteered at the All Saints Food Pantry on E. 129th Street. On a typical morning, the Pantry served about 80 families. Because Misty had been volunteering there since she started high school, she had come to know many of the people who came for help with getting food on the table.

One of them was Alphonses, who liked to be called Alphie. He was Hispanic and lived in a studio apartment shared with two cousins who had come to New York to find work. Alphie worked as a waiter in an upscale restaurant while he continued to go to auditions and work off-off-Broadway when he could.

That Saturday, two weeks before Christmas, the Pantry was giving out special holiday food boxes, complete with a turkey and all the other fixings for a Christmas meal.

"Thanks, Misty," he said as she handed him his food box. He was the last person in line that morning, having worked a double shift.

"How's it going, Alphie?" she asked, eager to gather any updates.

"Well, my agent gave me a call last night, letting me know I'm up for an audition first thing Monday."

"That's great! What's the part?"

"Something new that the Playwright's Initiative has been working on. I think it's a comedy."

"But what's the part?" Misty was a determined future journalist at heart.

"I don't know. My agent didn't offer much detail," he answered.

Alphie was being modest. His agent had told him the play had solid backing that could very well take it to Broadway. And Alphie wasn't just auditioning for a part; he was being considered for the lead. In between working double shifts and auditioning, Alphie was also taking care of a younger cousin, Marco, who had temporarily become homeless when his family was evicted from their apartment in the Bronx. The landlord wasn't about to spend money on restoring the boiler, so the city shut down the building to force the issue. Meanwhile, Marco's family, consisting of Dad, Mom, and three siblings, had been spread across the boroughs with relatives.

In a stroke of kismet, Marco was attending Cristo Rey on scholarship, where he was also a senior, having caught the eye of Misty. But you know how those teen-aged things go, especially when one party doesn't see the interest behind the beautiful green eyes of the other party of the female persuasion, who isn't about to spill the beans without some sort of prompting.

The following Monday, there was good reason for Misty to be distracted as she went through the lunch line.

"Good morning, sweetie," Mrs. Shevlin said as she scooped out a generous portion of a cheese casserole that was baked to perfection.

"Pardon me?" That was Misty's back-up response when her mind caught her elsewhere.

"Bless me, Father, for I have sinned," said Mrs. Shevlin, smiling at her own comeback. That was another thing that she couldn't quite understand about Catholicism. If you were going through the trouble of confessing your sins, why do it to a relative stranger? Hadn't they heard of Rosh Hashanah? Or why not go up to the person involved and ask forgiveness directly? Sure, it was harder, but it was a lot more effective in cutting down on the need to confess in the first place.

"Excuse me?" was all Misty could come up with.

"Earth to Misty. I'm teasing. You are really on another planet today, aren't you?"

"I'm sorry." Normally, Misty would have seen Mrs. Shevlin's retort as a wide-open opportunity to discuss the advantages of confession, but today, her brain was busy overprocessing information. Like the fact that she knew Alphie's waiter position was the only reliable source of income for the three cousins that were living with him. The apartment was in Alphie's name, and Marco was super-cute and trying really hard to blend in with the other seniors in hopes of salvaging as much of a senior year as possible. Which included a special Christmas week dance.

"What am I going to do?" Misty asked her best friend Rachel as they sat down to eat.

"Well, I guess we pick up our forks and begin tearing this amazing cheese casserole apart!" she answered, grinning from ear to ear. With that, she raised her glass of water to no one in particular. "I propose a toast to Mrs. Shevlin, the best lunch lady in all of Manhattan!" she said loudly.

Everyone else in the vicinity raised their glasses. With her eyes, Rachel cued Misty to raise hers as well. "Come on, slow-mo," she said, eyeing her friend for clues. Not finding any, she continued. "What's up?"

"Nothing."

"Don't say 'nothing' to me. I know better than that. I know you like the back of my hand. I know you better than you do, most days." With this, Rachel lightly touched her nose. "The nose knows all!"

"Yeah, so very true!" Misty laughed. She couldn't help it if Rachel's upbeat nature was the perfect foil for her own seriousness.

"Speak to me, kiddo!" Rachel was all ears. "It's a boy, isn't it?"

"No, it isn't." Misty was too quick to respond.

Rachel looked her right in the eye. "It's always a boy. Just tell me which one."

"It's not, honestly."

"Are you going to come clean, or do I have to stand up and make a public announcement that you have guy trouble?" She made a move to stand up.

"Calm down." Misty was an intensely private person, and the last thing she wanted was a public disclosure of any kind. "I'll tell you, but you're going to be really disappointed."

The frown on Rachel's face was deeper than a row in a farmer's field after spring plowing. "Just spill the beans. We've only got 15 minutes left to eat."

"You know Marco in our Shakespeare class?"

Rachel's frown vanished instantly at this tidbit. Only this morning Ms. Hasbrook had been reviewing the following lines he had penned:

Alas, that love, whose view is muffled still,
Should, without eyes, see pathways to his will?
Where shall we dine? Oh me – What fray was here?
Yet tell me not for I have heard it all.
Here's much to-do with hate, but more with love;

Why, then, oh brawling love! O loving hate!
O any thing, of nothing first created;
O heavy lightness! Serious vanity!
Misshapen chaos of well-seeming forms!
Feather of lead, bright smoke, cold fire, sick health!
Still-waking sleep, that is not what it is!

This love feel I, that feel no love in this.

"I don't like him that way."

"Methinks the lady doth protest too much!"

"I mean, it's just that I'm really interested in getting to know him, but he hardly sticks around long enough after school to get acquainted. And he doesn't seem interested much in socializing."

"You mean, he doesn't seem especially interested in socializing with you, right?"

"Bingo!"

"So, we have a 'Gee, I'd love to get to know this guy, but the school year is almost half over and a Christmas dance is coming up like a freight train, and it's like the most golden opportunity of all time, but I don't know him well enough to ask him out situation' on our hands?"

Misty raised her finger into the air for emphasis. "Exactly."

As if to add significance to Rachel's deduction, the bell signaling the end of the lunch break rang.

That night, Misty felt bad about slacking off on her evangelization efforts and said a prayer to St. Jude, asking for his assistance. After all, he was the supposed patron saint of lost causes, and she figured, if ever there was a lost cause, her chances with Marco surely qualified. Not one to hedge her bets, she followed up with a decade of the rosary before falling asleep.

Morning classes went quickly enough, leading to the lunch hour. And whatever Mrs. Shevlin was cooking up was a doozie because the aroma wafted its way through the entire school building. A mixture of roast meat, garlic, onion, cream sauce, and noodles. The rumor that started in the freshman homeroom, which was nearest to the cafeteria, was that it was beef stroganoff.

As the classes lined up for the midday meal, they seemed to be under the influence of whatever spices Mrs. Shevlin had used in creating her magnificent entrée. Normally, high schoolers would be talking about dating, sports, or the upcoming weekend. But not today.

"It's driving me crazy!" announced Rachel.

"Yeah, I can't put my finger on it either. It's not sage."

"Definitely not. It's too subtle for that," Misty agreed.

From the middle of the line, someone spoke out. "I got it. Coriander!"

Everyone turned to look at Soopretik, whose family was from India, to verify the spice. "I cannot say for certain, other than to say this is so unlike American cooking. It is making me homesick."

By the time Misty and Rachel had their plates filled, they could see it wasn't a stew dish. And it smelled absolutely divine.

"So, what's your secret?" Misty asked.

Mrs. Shevlin smiled. "Curry powder and coriander, and skip the Worcestershire sauce. And I added the sour cream to the noodles at the very end."

"So, it's not really a beef entrée, solo?"

"My child, it's much more than that! It's my own version of beef stroganoff."

"But the beef, it looks so tender, and it's shredded."

"That's because I had it in the slow cooker since six this morning, honey."

"Wow," said Rachel, beaming as her own plate was being filled. "I salute you on your culinary excellence!"

Mrs. Shevlin was bursting with happiness, and her cooking reflected that emotion. "Look, I'm trying something different today with the seniors."

Misty frowned. "Like what?"

I'm assigning seats for everyone. She looked at a handwritten chart she had taped to the steam table. "You're at table 4, and you'll find name tags there."

It turned out that Rachel was assigned to the same table, right across from Misty. Once they got there, they were thrown into the chaos of the senior section because of Mrs. Shevlin's random seating arrangement.

As Rachel sat down, her heart skipped a beat because the seat to her immediate right had been reserved for Marco. Her heart was still beating fast when Mrs. Shevlin left the serving line for a minute to walk over to the seniors and explain the arrangement.

"Look, you only have a few days left before Christmas break. Half the school year will be gone soon. I've been standing here noticing some of you hardly interact with each other, outside of your little cliques. So, I'm telling you, be a mensch and get to know your neighbor. You'll get a mitzvah if you do."

After this, Mrs. Shevlin caught Misty's eye, gave her a wink, and casually walked back to the serving line.

"Matchmaker, Matchmaker, catch me a catch," Rachel began singing under her breath.

"Cut it out!" Misty urgently whispered, with a slight kick strategically aimed at Rachel's legs under the table.

"Houston, we have a problem!" Rachel replied, just as Marco walked up to the table, found his name tag, and sat down next to Misty.

In between devouring Mrs. Shevlin's magnificent handiwork, Rachel spoke up. "So, Marco, how do you think The Bard would describe this meal we're eating?"

Marco paused, midway to putting another forkful into his mouth. He slowly put his silverware down and looked across the table at her. Tilting his head heavenward, he began, "Oh, what sweet morsels my mouth perceives. Be they a dream, they are as such! Tenderest of meats, succulent beyond description. Golden cream poured out upon fair noodles, embedded with such secret, sweet spices that I could not think of it without refraining from tears of joy. Pray tell, this elegant creation must be stolen from the table of the gods."

"Wow!" Rachel was duly impressed.

In response, he only gave a quick nod to her and said, "What's up, home fry?"

Which Misty found so funny that she spit out a portion of that very food in Marco's direction while trying to contain a laugh that came out of her at warp speed, sounding a bit like a pig's snort. She watched in horror as the smallest of portions landed on his shirt sleeve.

"I am so sorry! So very, very sorry!" was all Misty could say while turning a very bright shade of red.

Rachel's eyes widened as she put her hand to her mouth to avoid showing the huge smile that was settling on her face. Lucky for her, she was in between taking bites of the precious food.

Misty was thinking, "Great! I haven't spoken one word to Marco outside of class all semester, and the first thing I do when I'm sitting next to him is spew out my food on him like I'm an active volcano." She was wishing she had the ability to completely disappear. Either that, or shrink herself down to the size of a pea and roll away.

Macro looked at his left shirt sleeve, then at Misty with his bright, black eyes. And then a laugh began to emerge from deep inside him. Starting off small, it got bigger and bigger, growing alongside the smile on his face.

He held up both his hands in a useless effort to control himself. "Excuse me, please," he said, still looking at Misty. "But that was absolutely awesome!"

"What was awesome?" She was totally at a loss now.

"Your snort," he whispered to her. "You have that down one hundred percent."

In an effort to recover, she picked up her napkin and began to clean up the food on Marco's shirt.

"That's okay," he said, putting his hand on top of hers to stop the clean-up operation, which only caused Misty's heart to go into triple overtime. "Wow, I can't believe he actually touched me," she was thinking. "How very cool is that? I mean, in a strictly non-romantic, platonic sort of way."

Marco continued, "Aren't we in the same Shakespeare class?"

For some reason, Misty found her brain temporarily unavailable. Rachel came to her rescue. "Yes. She is. All three of us are in it."

Marco nodded. Misty's brain continued to be on hold.

"So, isn't it interesting that Mrs. Shevlin had us sitting together like this?" Rachel administered a swift kick to Misty to jump-start her into being part of the conversation.

"Yeah, I don't get it, but you can't really discount her culinary expertise. I mean, the woman is an absolute genius," Marco said.

"What is going on here?" Misty thought. From the time she was born, she was forced to talk with adults because her parents had two kids, 15 years apart from each other. Misty was their "surprise" child, entering the world four years after her older brother had left home. She might as well have been an only kid because her memories of him were of a series of postcards he sent as he traveled the country, working construction jobs.

In response to her brother's exit, she became the center of attention. But she never took advantage of their generosity. Throughout her childhood, Misty had made it a personal goal never to upset the apple cart. Yet, being the youngest, she absorbed everything in sight, being especially perceptive. To the point of remembering details that would fly by other people at the speed of light. Like the fact that Marco always rubbed his right earlobe in class just before he was about to let go with a zinger. He had done that a few moments ago before calling Rachel a home fry.

"Yep, no doubt!" Misty blurted the words out, which was atypical for her normal, slow, thoughtful delivery.

"Are you okay?" Marco was a free spirit with a generous heart, and he naturally reached out to Misty to help put her at ease. He looked straight at Misty before continuing. "You have the most gorgeous green eyes."

"I'm fine, and thanks," she said. "I'm Finnish on my mom's side. That's where the green eyes come from."

Misty wanted so badly to let Marco know that she knew his cousin, Alphie. She wanted to tell him that she admired the way his family looked out for each other, but she figured it wouldn't be proper to mention anything about knowing him through the All Saints Food Pantry.

As if reading her mind, Marco picked up. "Alphie knows you. He talks about you every time he comes back from the Pantry. He says you always have a smile and ask him how his auditions are going. You treat him like a human being, not like a poor person."

"That's because Alphie isn't poor. He's an amazing guy who loves his family, and that includes you."

Marco gently put his hand on Misty's again. "Yeah, Alphie is the best," Marco said softly.

Ever the clever one, Rachel seized the moment to continue setting a Shakespearean theme by quoting:

My flesh is soft and plump, my marrow burning;
My smooth moist hand, were it with thy hand felt,
Would if thy palm dissolve, or seem to melt.

"You probably already have a date lined up for the Christmas dance?" he asked.

"Actually, she doesn't" Rachel piped in enthusiastically.

Misty kicked her friend again. This time a little harder, before admitting, "She's right. I don't."

"Would you like to go with me?"

A smile exploded on Misty's face. "Yes!"

And at that very moment, Mrs. Shevlin walked up to table 4. She couldn't help it. From the serving line, it seemed like things were going well, but she wanted confirmation.

"So, how's it going at this table?" She asked.

Misty's smile was still on her face. "Merry Christmas, Mrs. Shevlin!"

"And Happy Hanukkah to you, too!" she said, laughing.

Missy Gets Dancing Lessons

"I'd like to look like a wife with two kids who's been married for ten years and been in love every single day of it."

—*Boo*, by Rene Gutteridge (used with permission from the author)

It was December 14, and Missy Southfield wanted to feel in love. She sat in a pew on a side aisle of the church, openly weeping. She had asked her husband to take their children home so that she could have a moment after the service to compose herself.

She hadn't really gone to church that morning with that in mind, but Pastor Mitchell's teaching had a delayed reaction, hitting home during the closing greeting. His encouragement to the congregation to linger over coffee and doughnuts in the fellowship hall quickly cleared the sanctuary, leaving Missy alone until Shirley, Pastor Mitchell's wife, spotted Missy and slid up next to her.

"It's nice to have a quiet time, isn't it?" Shirley asked.

Missy nodded.

Shirley was in her late 50s, and her own children were grown. She and her husband were just beginning to experience the joys of being empty nesters. Missy's kids were teenagers with more than a few years left at home.

Pastor Mitchell had been teaching on Jesus, mentioning the greatest commandment. He was using Mark 12:30-31 as his text. (A religious leader asked Jesus: "Of all the commandments, which is the most important?" Jesus answered: "Love the Lord your God with all your heart and with all your soul and with all your mind and with all your strength. The second is this: Love your neighbor as yourself. There is no commandment greater than these.")

"When it comes to the bottom line, Jesus was saying it's very simple. And that's good news!" Pastor Mitchell had told the congregation. "This season, we'll be celebrating God's mercy and grace and deep, unconditional love. That love is for every single one of us!"

"I don't want to miss it," Missy said to Shirley.

"Miss what?"

"The joy of the holiday season! I don't want to go through Christmas focused on obligations."

"It's a busy time of year, isn't it?" Shirley sympathized.

Missy nodded. "With the kids' school and extracurriculars. And it probably doesn't help that I'm working part-time to help us catch up on bills."

As soon as the words left her mouth, the smell of evergreens emanating from the Scotch pines set along the front of the sanctuary triggered a memory.

Missy was ten years old, and it was Christmas Day. There was snow on the ground – about four inches of it. More than enough to head to Kindleberger Park, which was only a block away from where the family lived in Parchment, Michigan.

"Dad, can we go sledding after church?" she asked, eyes bright and pleading.

He smiled at her. "Sure, sweetheart. We've got to burn off that great breakfast that your mom made anyway, right?"

She gave her dad the thumbs up.

The service at the United Methodist Church flew by. The sermon time was eaten up by a repeat performance of the kids' Christmas Pageant from Christmas Eve, which was shortened. Once the pastor introduced the pageant, they cut to the manger. Missy was a shepherd that year. She felt honored to be looking over the flock, until Robbie Blackford spilled the beans at school.

"So, what's it feel like being the shepherd?" he had asked her during lunch.

"What are you talking about?" Missy answered back.

"The Christmas Pageant. Everyone knows about it," he smiled.

"I doubt that anyone cares."

"Oh, I wouldn't say that," Robbie said, moving a little closer. (Robbie was the class snitch. Over his career in elementary school, he had honed the art of tattling to perfection.)

"Why in the world would you be the slightest bit interested in a Christmas pageant?" she said to him, tilting her head sideways to drive home the point.

"I have my reasons."

"Can you give me a for instance?"

"For instance, it'd be pretty embarrassing if the whole class found out that you flubbed your lines."

"But I haven't flubbed my lines. I know them by heart."

Robbie slowly shook his head. "Hearsay."

"What do you mean?"

"It's a shame how rumors get started," said Robbie. "It's really awful how people will believe whatever they hear if it's repeated often enough."

"But I'm a reasonable person," Robbie lifted his hands, palms up, as if he was a pint-sized version of "The Closer." "All you have to do is get me in as a substitute sheep."

"Pardon?"

"Just ask your pageant director if I can be a sheep. They never have enough sheep."

"And what if I don't?" Missy challenged.

Robbie slowly shook his head, then looked Missy in the eye. "It's a shame how rumors go around, isn't it?"

So, bowing to social pressure, Missy asked the pageant director if it would be possible to add a sheep to make it an even half-dozen. The director agreed, knowing that the sheep had no lines to learn, other than "Baa."

On Christmas Eve, Robbie had shown up on time, was given the proper costume, and told where to sit on all fours, with the other sheep around the manger.

The pageant proceeded without incident. Until the very end, at the climactic moment when everyone was gathered around the manger in adoration. It was good enough for a Christmas card photo, but in the seconds before the choir director came out to lead the congregation in "Hark! The Herald Angels Sing," Robbie stood up, hoisted his right hoof into the air, and shouted, "Peace out!"

This normally wouldn't have been much of a problem, but his exclamation shocked the sheep next to him into falling into the nearest sheep, and in short order, the domino effect took its full course, causing all the sheep to wind up sprawled out on the floor of the nativity scene.

She had immediately confessed to the pageant director, who miraculously forgave Missy in between her tears.

It was a little puzzling to Missy why on earth her brain would choose to recall such a Christmas memory until she realized that Pastor Mitchell's sermon was a powerful encouragement about the power of love.

Shirley turned to Missy. "Are you okay?" bringing her back to the present day.

Missy shook her head.

"We all are short-sighted in our thinking sometimes," Shirley said.

Missy turned away from Shirley, ashamed. "I'm talking about something deeper."

Shirley moved a little closer. "Can you help me understand?"

"A lot of time, I go around thinking that my point of view is the only one that's right, and it complicates things."

"Having two kids and maintaining a household and working part-time is hard. It's bound to take a toll. Being pulled in so many directions."

"Those are symptoms but not the cause." Missy was sitting straight and upright in the pew.

"I'm sorry if I'm not offering much for you to grab hold of."

For the first time since they began their conversation, Missy turned to Shirley and smiled.

"It's not you," Missy said. "It's me. I can't give what I don't have."

Shirley's eyes expressed nothing but empathy. "And what don't you have?"

Missy laughed out loud. It was a good thing the sanctuary of the church had emptied, and most of the congregation were either chatting outside or headed to the fellowship hall for donuts and coffee.

"I'm not really sure I can put my finger on it," Missy tried to respond. "It's complicated, and it's embarrassing to have to admit I'm prone to selfish behavior."

"We all are, Missy. Please don't let that cloud your understanding."

"Oh, I think I understand. That's the problem."

If only she had half the bravery she'd exhibited after that fateful Christmas Pageant years ago.

After her confession to the pageant director, Missy had walked over to Robbie and pulled him aside. They still had their costumes on.

"Hey, what kind of a stunt was that?" she demanded.

"What? You didn't like my little proclamation?" Robbie was beside himself with self-adulation.

"You trainwrecked the performance!"

"Wasn't it awesome?"

"If it weren't Christmas, I'd sock you one!"

Missy was getting hot under the collar. So much so that she had to take off the shepherd's cloak she was wearing to get some fresh air to keep from passing out. Robbie followed her lead, taking off his sheep's head.

"I was only having a little fun," he tried to explain.

"What you did went beyond having fun, Robbie! You need to understand something."

"Like what?"

"Like hurting a whole group of kids with your scheme is thoughtless, and unless you want to grow up friendless and lonely, you should knock it off. Not to mention what God thinks about the subject."

Robbie arranged his face into a giant squint, trying to appear threatening. "You think you know what's going on in God's brain?"

Missy let out a slow, deep breath before answering. "Read Proverbs sometime. It's full of what happens to idiots."

"Proverbs?"

"It's in the Old Testament."

Unfortunately, Missy didn't grow up to become an expert at confrontation. She usually avoided it. Which takes us back to why she was sitting in the church with Shirley with Christmas so close you could smell the gingerbread cookies baking.

"Why do we put so much emphasis on our own opinions?" Missy was trying her best to continue the conversation.

"None of us likes to think we're wrong." Shirley responded.

Missy only shook her head.

Shirley gently put her hand on Missy's. "You seem to have quite a lot on your mind. Moving from one thought to another."

"And not making much sense of it!" Missy smiled.

"Well, sometimes life just doesn't make sense. It doesn't add up logically, no matter how hard we try to make it so."

"Do you think God is always logical?" Missy asked.

Shirley paused for a moment. "I'm not sure. Logic implies understanding, and we're really at a disadvantage, being very limited beings trying to purse a limitless one."

"Tell me about it!"

"Just because we don't understand the reason behind an action doesn't mean it isn't logical. What's the scripture about God saying God's ways aren't our ways? Or that God's thoughts are as far from ours as the east is from the west?"

"Christmas is a perfect example!" Missy blurted out.

"Pardon?"

"I mean, what is at all logical about the Creator of the Universe caring enough about us to intervene to re-establish a relationship after we pretty much cut it off? The logical thing would have been to kick Adam and Eve out of the Garden and then be done with it."

"Or start over with a new pair!" Shirley was on a roll.

"I never would have thought of that option. Just cut your losses and start again from scratch."

"Actually, now that I think of it, there were at least two other times when God was severely ready to do exactly that," Shirley continued.

"Really?"

"Sure. Remember Sodom and Gomorrah with Abraham bargaining God down so that God wouldn't kill off the entire human race? And then five centuries later, the same sort of thing happened with Moses."

"You're right! I don't exactly know what that has to do with Christmas, but you're right." Missy responded.

"Maybe the whole idea is to concentrate on Emmanuel."

"What's that?"

"God with us. That's what Emmanuel means. Try focusing on the babe and the fact that God is dwelling with us, with you. God actively chose to live with you," said Shirley.

Missy let out a sigh. "That's almost incomprehensible. In theory I accept it, but the day-to-day stuff tarnishes it. I keep messing up, over and over. Stumbling over the same things."

"That's the beautiful mystery of the incarnation. It takes off the tarnish of daily life so we can breathe." She paused a moment before continuing. "The stories of the Garden of Eden and Abraham and Moses are stories of second chances. The Bible is full of real people, just like you and me. We can trip and mess up, but God invites us to fall in love again!"

"But how can you keep everyday life from happening?"

Shirley began to talk about Brother Lawrence, a monk living in France in the 1500s. And how he slowly learned to bring God into the center of things.

"He called it practicing the presence of God," she explained.

"Was he working part-time with two kids?" Missy asked, raising her eyebrows.

Shirley laughed. "He worked in the kitchen of a monastery, and that meant helping to fix three meals a day for all those monks. 365 days a year."

"So, what was his secret?"

"His secret was he kept it simple. He said, 'I began to live as if there was nothing but God and I in the world.'"

"No gimmicks, huh?"

Shirley shook her head. "Believe it or not, he came to the point where he began to see everyday life as a series of opportunities to get closer to God."

"And it worked?" Missy asked with eyes pleading. "Even in the kitchen?"

"It absolutely worked." Shirley smiled before continuing. "And since we're sitting here in a Methodist church, you know about Susanna Wesley?"

Missy shook her head.

"Well, she and her husband had nineteen kids. This was around the 1700s, and ten of them survived. I can't imagine the pain of having lost that many children. And then being a mom in a busy household. It got to the point where Susanna had a rule. When she put a sheet over her head, her kids knew their mom was praying, and they needed to leave her alone."

"Did it work?"

Shirley nodded. "Two of those kids grew up to be John and Charles Wesley. One wrote over six thousand hymns. The other founded the Methodist church."

"Then maybe there's hope for me?"

Shirley took Missy's hand. "The very fact that you tarried behind after service today proves that your soul is already nudging your heart in that direction. All you need to do is follow God's lead."

Missy began to cry softly.

"Do you think that God's good at ballroom dancing? I'd love to get my husband and me to take lessons, but right now, we can't afford it."

Shirley took a pencil from the pew and a connection card. She turned it over and began to write something, handing it over to Missy.

"This is the address and phone number of the Congregational Church downtown. They host dancing classes on Mondays. It's usually $4 a lesson, but we can cover you."

"What do you mean 'cover you'?"

"It's a present from our church family to yours. Dancing lessons for three months. To help get you through the rest of winter."

Now Missy's tears came harder.

"Thank you! You have no idea! Thank you for listening!"

Shirley gave Missy a hug before they both stood up. "That's what we're here for, isn't it?"

"I suppose so," Missy said, blowing her nose. "But I never really thought I'd be the one needing assistance."

"Sometimes it's hard to actually ask. Or we think we need to figure it all out for ourselves. But nothing could be further from the truth," said Shirley. "We're all in this together. We just need to accept the invitation."

Missy smiled. "Thanks for the reminder!"

Shirley gave Missy a hug. "Merry Christmas!"

Ruby's Present

Ruby was standing across the room at the office party watching Sammy give a pretty good imitation of someone having a great time. His full name was Samuel, but no one called him that. He had quite a reputation as being a ladies' man, which was ironic when you considered how he treated them.

But the point wasn't actually Sammy, or even holiday office parties like this one. Ruby had invested ten years of her life in the organization, and at the moment, she was feeling every minute of it. She had been hired straight out of college with a degree in social research. Most of her classmates had gotten jobs with marketing firms. She had chosen to go against the grain, working for an advocacy group focused on environmental issues.

Gretel Markowitz had spotted Ruby and casually walked up to her. "Nice party, huh?"

"The best, if you're trying to establish a low-tide mark in your social life."

The remark had caused a deep frown to appear on Gretel's forehead. They were officemates who shared adjoining cubicles.

"Do you want to go somewhere and talk about it?"

The fact was that Ruby rarely shared personal information at work. Or anywhere else. She had grown up with parents who barely spoke to each other. There was very little parental guidance to speak of, which at first suited Ruby very well. Until other kids in the neighborhood told her how their parents were involved in their lives.

Ruby shook her head and offered a weak smile. "Don't mind me. It's just the season."

"But it's the time for tidings of comfort and joy!" Gretel was being sincere about that. For her, Thanksgiving to Christmas was the apex of the entire year. The fact that she hung out at the local synagogue didn't deter her from enjoying the perks of Christianity.

"Why would you say that? You're still searching for the Messiah, right?"

"That doesn't mean I can't appreciate a good thing when I see it."

"What's that, exactly?"

"Slowing down and appreciating what the Eternal One's given us."

Normally, Ruby wasn't given to sarcasm, but the glass of red wine that was inside her had already begun to lubricate the inhibitions right out of her. "You sound like a Girl Scout."

"Pardon?"

Ruby motioned towards one of the outer offices usually inhabited by executives. They walked in and shut the door.

"I was saying you sound like a salesman for the Good Living Institute of America."

Once again Gretel frowned. She was hired only half a year after Ruby, so the two of them had ample opportunity to get to know each other. But Ruby had done a very good job of sidetracking any conversation that approached the subject of personal belief. So, Gretel knew nothing of the deep disappointment that her officemate held in regard to things religious. She didn't know what it felt like to grow up with bickering adults too worn out from fighting with each other to steer their children in any sort of spiritual direction. She didn't know what it was like to rely on the input of neighborhood kids as to what place of worship they attended. (And it was usually these same children who invited Ruby to come with them to the assorted places that they frequented.)

After a while, those houses of worship began to blend into each other. As far as Ruby was concerned, they were minor variations on a theme of trying to get the congregations lulled into a false sense of security. She would have preferred an open question-and-answer period. She appreciated some of the worship songs for their melody, but the lyrics flew right by her, so she kept silent. How could she sing out what she didn't believe?

Gretel chose her words carefully before responding. "Help me understand what happened that makes you so turned off about Christmas."

"It's more like what didn't happen."

"For instance?"

On any other day, Ruby would have easily deflected such a direct question. This time, the whole irony of the situation was weighing too heavily on her to ignore.

"I don't like pretending," she said. "It starts with Thanksgiving when we all sit down and eat too much and pretend to be thankful, which is bad enough. But Christmas only takes it up a notch, and we're supposed to pretend that a baby was born who grew up to save the world."

"Maybe some of us believe it," Gretel said.

"Do you?" Ruby's green eyes were staring directly into Gretel's.

"Most of it, except the part about the Savior being born. I'm still waiting for that one. Meanwhile, I hedge my bets by celebrating Yom Kippur and asking the Eternal One for forgiveness."

"You're hedging your bets by believing in a supreme being?"

"I was trying to lighten you up a little! I'm not in it solely for the taking away of sins anymore."

"Then what's the attraction?" Ruby asked.

"The bitter herbs and unleavened bread at Passover." Gretel said this with a straight face.

"Pardon?"

"Ruby, I'm joking, okay? It's a Jewish tradition passed on from ancient times when my ancestors were lost and wandering in the desert."

"What's so funny about that?"

"Most humor is born out of irony. And forty years of hunkering down with sand fleas every night, eating manna three times a day when you could have easily decided to stop complaining, and stop forgetting who the Eternal One was and let Him lead you to the Promised Land is highly ironic."

"That's interesting, but you still haven't answered my question," Ruby countered.

Luckily for Ruby, Gretel was named after her great-grandmother whose mother grew up a few miles away from the Black Forest and was a huge fan of fairy tales. She also loved to go for walks in the woods. At a young age, she was told about a creator and having already experienced much of the creation, it was easy for her young faith to grow. Although the Torah eventually replaced the Brothers Grimm, she still appreciated their creativity.

"My grandmother loved fairy tales."

"Are you making this up as you go along to deliberately bring out the sarcasm?" Ruby asked.

"I'm trying to tell you something if you'll slow down the 'I hate Christmas' freight train long enough to listen."

Ruby laughed out loud at that one. "The floor's yours."

Gretel sat down, and Ruby followed her lead. Once they were both comfortable, she continued. "My grandmother knew how to believe. She got it from my great-grandmother, who lived near the Black Forest."

Gretel took a deep breath before continuing. "I mean, our family has always been Jewish, on both sides, as far back as we can trace. But there was a deeper spiritual dimension to my great-grandmother that rubbed off on my grandma. And Mom passed it on to me."

"You mean like the Kabbalah?"

Gretel shook her head. "This was much simpler. It's about the ability to hope in someone outside of ourselves that the Eternal One brings and our ability to trust."

"That sounds exactly like a fairy tale to me."

"But it isn't, because it's real," Gretel said.

"I'm going to give you a huge benefit of the doubt and ask you to explain yourself."

"There's no explanation for it."

"What!"

"There's no explanation for it because it requires faith."

"That's preposterous."

"Is it?"

"Yes!"

"Then let me ask you a question. And you have to promise to answer it honestly," Gretel said.

"Shoot."

"Where do you place your faith?"

"I don't place it anywhere because I don't have it," Ruby said.

"Yes, you do."

"No, I don't, Gretel."

"Everyone has faith in someone or something. We're built to have it. Like a moral GPS. Even if you're saying you don't have it, by default you're saying you have faith in nothing but yourself."

"So that's where all my sarcasm comes from?"

"There's a good chance of it."

"That's so convenient. I'm denying my need for faith and body-slamming my moral compass. Is that it?"

Gretel decided to try another avenue.

"Have you heard of Brandon Manning?" she asked. (Gretel was referring to an author and reluctant theologian who held that God's love was the most important thing a person needed to experience to come into relationship with God. And that, in the end, it served no purpose to try to differentiate among various Christian denominations because we were all once spiritual urchins anyway. What was the point of trying to make yourself look better than anyone else, because God knew exactly who we were in the first place?)

Ruby shook her head, "No."

"He wrote *The Ragamuffin Gospel*."

"I'm sorry, but I'm not familiar with it."

"Well, it's an interesting way to look at the relationship between Jesus, the church, and God."

"What's Manning's main point?" Ruby was rapidly losing interest.

"One point was that the church in America really wasn't a church of grace."

"What's that got to do with faith?" Ruby asked.

"You can't really have one without the other."

"I think it depends on your definition of grace."

"Unearned favor. A pure gift," answered Gretel.

Ruby's eyes widened. If there was a word that defined her character, it was practical. She got her first job at 10 by offering to clean her neighbor's garage. For a kid, she had an innate knack for sorting through clutter. Growing up, her side of the bedroom, which she shared with an older sister, was remarkably clean. Her toys were always put back in her toy box after she played with them. Her books were sorted neatly and alphabetically by author on a small bookshelf she had.

Ruby was the kind of girl who had her school clothes set out the night before. She had heard about procrastination, but really couldn't grasp that something like 97 percent of the world operated that way. She was Type A+ and proud of it.

"Your definition of grace sounds sloppy. Like something the lunch lady plops on your plate on Monday as you go through the food line," Ruby said.

"You want to know what Manning says is the first question that God will ask us when we die?"

"You're going back to the Ragamuffin guy?" Ruby asked.

"Yes."

"Tell me."

"God's going to look us in the eye and ask, 'Did you let me love you?'"

"Score one for free will, right?" Ruby put her hands up, mimicking a referee calling a field goal. Then she began to cry.

"What's wrong?" Gretel ached to reach out to her workmate.

What was wrong was that, suddenly, Ruby began to feel all the "slings and arrows of outrageous fortune" when it came to her experience with the opposite sex. It didn't help that there had been very little parental influence or wisdom handed out to temper her life experience. If anything, her life had taught her to keep her feelings bottled inside because it was much safer that way, with no emotional mess to clean up. As far as Ruby was concerned, "nothing ventured, nothing gained" should never have been misinterpreted to include relationships.

"It's nothing," Ruby said.

"Oh, it's something, alright. I've worked in the next cubicle over from you long enough to know that your normal mode of operation is to keep to yourself. So much so that it'd take a stick of dynamite to loosen you out of your shell. Right now, compared to your so-called normal self, you're like a volcano about to erupt."

"No offense, Gretel, but you don't know me well enough to say that."

Gretel moved a bit closer and gently spoke: "But I'd like to. For heaven's sake, Ruby, you've got to open up to someone around here. We spend more time at work than anywhere else. It's a great place to start."

"What is happening here?" Ruby thought. She had no decent work-related friendships to guide her through this conversation. She realized that Gretel was reaching out, and there was a part of her that wanted to become engaged, but there was a deeper part that was frozen in a sea of uncertainty.

"It's okay not to know how it's going to turn out," Gretel offered.

"What?"

"It's okay not to know the next step because you should know the end of the story."

"I should?"

Gretel nodded. "God wins. Hope wins. Faith wins. Because love wins."

Instead of saying something ultra-cynical, Ruby felt the frozen sea inside her starting to melt.

She barely whispered her response. "I want love to win."

"Then from this point forward, keep asking God to help you trust," said Gretel.

"You think it's really that simple?"

"It's about the hardest thing you'll ever have to do, but I'm pretty sure you've found that the alternative is even harder."

No sooner had the words gotten out of Gretel's mouth than Sammy knocked on the office widow, smiling, and trying to invite himself in.

Gretel looked at him and shook her head, "No."

In response, Sammy picked up a piece of paper, grabbed a magic marker, and wrote furiously, then slipped the message underneath the door. It read, "I'm a fun guy!"

Ruby turned the paper over, picked up a pen, scribbled "That's not good enough, sorry!" and slipped it back to him.

Sammy scratched out Ruby's retort, wrote something, and slammed the paper against the glass. "Your loss, ladies!" He then smirked, did an about-face, and walked away.

"You know, I used to think that guys like Sammy were actually worth going after," Ruby said.

"Disappointment really clouds a person's vision, doesn't it?"

"It's tough coming up empty at the end of the day," Gretel sighed. "Which gets us back to the main point of this Christmas party conversation, but I need to grab something from my cubicle. Hold on a minute."

Gretel stretched, opened the door, and walked out. Within a couple of minutes, she was back.

"You needed your purse to continue our chat?" asked Ruby, raising her eyebrows in disbelief.

Gretel reached in and pulled out her copy of *The Ragamuffin Gospel*. She opened it up and pointed to a section towards the very end of the book called "A Word After."

"Here," she said, putting her finger firmly down on the page. Read this."

Gretel picked up the book and began to read out loud:

The love of God is simply unimaginable. 'May Christ dwell in your hearts through faith, and may love be the root and foundation of your life. Thus, you will be able to grasp fully, with all the holy ones, the breadth and length and height and depth of Christ's love, and experience this love which surpasses all knowledge, so that you may attain to the fullness of God himself' (Ephesians 3:17-19).

Do we really hear what Paul is saying? Stretch, man stretch! Let go of impoverished, circumscribed, and finite perceptions of God. The love of Christ is beyond all knowledge, beyond anything we can intellectualize or imagine. It is not a mild benevolence but a consuming fire. Jesus is so unbearably forgiving, so infinitely patient and so unendingly loving that He provides us with the resources we need to live lives of gracious response. 'Glory be to him whose power, working in us, can do infinitely more than we can ask or imagine.' (Ephesians 3:20).

Does it sound like an easy religion?

Gretel slowly put the book down as Ruby answered Manning's question: "No, it doesn't. Not when you look at it like that."

Gretel smiled. "Yeah, I should talk. I'm not even a gentile, but I'm beginning to get it. I mean, for us, it's highly ironic that Saul of Tarsus, a Pharisee among Pharisees, grew up to become the Paul who wrote the book of Ephesians. We know that there's a Messiah, we just haven't been convinced that He has come yet." She paused before continuing. "So, like Manning said: Are you going to let God love you?"

Slowly, a grin began to spread across Ruby's face. Unlike any smile she'd ever had, because this one was coming from deep within her as she slowly nodded her head yes.

"Merry Christmas, Gretel!" she said, giving her friend a hug.

"Shalom to you, too!" Ruby said.

Saree to the Rescue

Effie sat down in the front row of the sanctuary. She was new to the city and had naturally gravitated towards St. Malachy's Church on West 49th Street. Being Monday morning, the sanctuary was empty but open to anyone who might have been so inclined to enter.

It had been quite the adventure to make the move from Burlington, Michigan, to New York City. I mean, why does someone move that far from a town that hasn't changed in over 100 years? Even if you were the class valedictorian (which Effie was), and even if you got lucky and attended Hope College on a full academic scholarship.

Ten years of working for the *Coldwater Daily Reporter* had paid the rent, but one day, when Andy Omstead, the editor, assigned her to cover a cow who had wandered into the Seventh Day Adventist's Community Room on a slow news day, she drew the line.

"No," she spoke up.

"What?"

"I said, no. I'm not doing it, Andy."

He laughed before continuing. "If memory serves me, it's usually the editor who tells the reporter what to cover. Last time I checked, I was the editor. How hard can it be? Get out there to the church before the cow wanders off, take the photo, come up with a snappy cutline, and get back here."

"That's not the point."

"Oh, I would say it's exactly the point, Effie. My job isn't to convince you to take an assignment. Especially one that's handed to you on a silver platter."

"A cow story is a silver platter?"

"Yeah. Especially in Branch County on a Monday when nothing much is happening. Grab a camera and get moving."

But Effie didn't follow instructions. She didn't follow Andy's lead at all. And as a matter of fact, she just sat there laughing.

"What's this?" Andy frowned.

"This is the part when I tell you I quit," said Effie as she grabbed her jacket, stood up, and walked toward the front door.

"Where in the world do you think you're going without the camera?"

Andy was having a hard time believing that his most seasoned reporter was making a break for the great unknown. Especially when he figured he had given her tomorrow's front-page photo.

"It's been real." Effie smiled, trying to soften the blow. "Honestly, it's been fun. But I'm not in the mood to take a picture of a cow."

"It's not just any cow," he tried arguing with her. "It's a cow that's currently keeping the Seventh Day Adventist's fellowship team from fixing a funeral luncheon."

"Minor inconvenience," she told him.

"It's news!" he yelled after her as she walked out the door.

Two days later, she boarded a train for New York City. Effie wasn't one to beat around the bush.

Of course, she had called Cindy Scholtman, her best friend, before heading to the airport. Cindy had moved to Brooklyn eight years before the hipsters did, so she had landed an affordable place on Bushwick Avenue.

Effie had begun to use St. Malachy's as her Manhattan touchstone because it was in Midtown and close to enough publishing houses and media outlets.

So, here she was, absorbing the peace and quiet of the sanctuary at a time of day when it stood in direct contrast to the hustle and bustle of the city outside its doors.

Her thoughts were interrupted by the remembrance of a conversation she and Cindy had the night Effie moved in.

"So, where's the nearest church around here?" Effie had begun, fully knowing her friend wasn't much of a churchgoer under normal circumstances.

"Couldn't tell you."

"Are you still angry with God?"

"Did you come all the way to Brooklyn to harass me?" she teased, lifting her eyebrows to emphasize she was only partly kidding.

"No, but it's been twelve years since your sister passed." They had been two years apart, with Cindy being the eldest.

"Yes, it has, and I miss her every day. Every day, I wake up and wonder, what would Becky look like now? Would her hair still be blonde? Or would it have eventually darkened? Would she have been an education major in college and teaching in an elementary school now? That's all she ever talked about."

In Cindy's experience, precious few of her classmates knew from early on what exactly they had been put on this earth for, and Becky was one of them.

Effie's attitude softened. "I know you were close."

"I was her older sister. I was supposed to be the one to protect her."

"There was no way you could have kept her from getting in a car with friends coming home from school. She did that every day. How can anyone predict that a drunk driver would run a stop sign and totally broadside another car?"

Cindy shook her head. "I was going to pick her up that day. I told her I'd meet her right after school because I had Mom's car. She wasn't supposed to be riding home with friends that afternoon."

"Things happen. How would you know that swinging by the pharmacy to pick up a prescription would cause a 15-minute delay? That wasn't your doing."

"That's not the point," Cindy countered. "God knew there was a drunken driver on the road that afternoon. God knew I'd be late, and that Becky had a ton of friends who would offer her a ride home. God's omniscient, right?"

"Not in the sense that you're getting at."

"Are you making excuses for an omnipotent being?" Cindy's eyes were flashing. "How ironic."

"It's not ironic; it's life," Effie answered back. "Life is full of 'what ifs' and God isn't always going to make it easy for us and eliminate those situations."

"How convenient."

"It's not convenience. It's painful, and it hurts, but it's the very sort of thing that can cause us to go deeper into relationship with God."

Cindy slowly shook her head. "Or else lose whatever faith we had to begin with."

In the quiet of the sanctuary, Effie was thinking, "What else could I have said to comfort my friend?"

Effie realized that Becky's death wasn't merely a stumbling block. It was evidence of a huge chasm that existed between Cindy's soul and God. Before heading out for a scheduled interview at *The New Yorker*, she said a quick prayer for her friend.

As she headed down 42nd Street, she was full of anticipation. So what if the job were an entry-level fact-checker?

Effie was all efficiency when she sat down with the non-fiction editor, whose name was Corie.

"So," Corie began, as she looked at the notes she had written on Effie's resume, "I see you have a strong background in print journalism."

"I worked for a daily for ten years as a hard-news reporter."

"What was the circulation?"

"A little over five thousand."

"Your former editor said that you could really churn out the copy." Corie paused, wrinkling her brow before looking up at Effie. "He also said that you refused to cover a cow story. What was that about?"

Effie couldn't help but laugh. "It was a slow news day," she tried to explain. "A very slow news day." She leaned forward and spoke, almost in a whisper. "Have you ever tried to interview a cow?"

Corie smiled. "When I first moved here, I was working for the *Daily News,* and I was assigned to cover a family of ducks who had climbed onto the Rockaway Beach subway platform."

"At least it was newsworthy."

"It was the same morning as 9/11. I was sent out at 8 AM to cover the ducks. By the time I got to Rockaway, the whole City had been shut down. I'd never felt so useless in my whole life."

Effie had nothing but sympathy. "That's the news business for you."

"We're looking for a fact-checker," Corie continued. "We pride ourselves on taking the time to ensure accuracy."

"Mistakes drive me crazy."

She got the job.

As soon as she was in the lobby, Effie reached for her cell phone and called Cindy.

"Hey, do you have a minute?" As luck would have it, Cindy did. She was an assistant curator at the Museum of the City of New York and was about to head out the door to Columbia University to borrow some of their archived photos.

"Sure, what's up?"

"You are speaking with the newest fact-checker at *The New Yorker*! I am so excited!"

"Wow! That's amazing!"

"Yeah. The only downside is that the editor I'm working with made it clear that I can't submit any copy of my own for at least a year. She wants me to concentrate on my job."

"Be that as it may, what a coup for small-town America!"

Effie laughed. "I guess. So, how does small town America celebrate when something like this happens?" Then an idea came to her in a flash. "Are you up for doing something fun on a Saturday morning?"

"Of course, as long as it's legal."

"Good. I'll fill you in when I get home tonight."

That night Cindy had Chinese takeout on the dining room table ready for supper.

After Effie told Cindy about the particulars of her new job, she changed the subject.

"So, about celebrating on Saturday. I was wondering, will you trust me with taking you somewhere that's right here in Brooklyn?"

Cindy nodded her approval.

"It's only a subway stop away."

That Saturday the two of them headed out the door towards the "J" train at 8:15. It gave them plenty of time to get to the home of Metro World Ministries. Effie had heard about the children's ministry when their senior pastor had come to her home church a few years ago.

Once Cindy discovered they were walking towards a church building, she balked.

"You didn't say anything about going to church!" she said.

"We're not exactly going to church," said Effie. "We're going to Kids' Saturday Sunday School."

"What?"

"Metro has an awesome street ministry to kids," she explained. "On Saturday they host a gigantic Sunday School."

"But it's still church, isn't it?"

Effie smiled. "Not like any you've experienced! And because this is their final Saturday before Christmas, they'll do six sessions today. I called the volunteer coordinator, and she said we could help with getting the kids back on the buses in-between sessions."

No sooner did they walk into the parking lot when a series of buses came pulling in, each carrying 20 to 30 kids. The staff and volunteers were all wearing bright yellow Yogi Bear t-shirts, which identified the ministry.

Effie, with her reporter's determination, went straight to the nearest volunteer.

"Excuse me, I called the volunteer coordinator, and she told us to come to observe today, but we're good to go if you could use some help."

"Yes!" she said, with a grateful smile. "If you could take these magic markers and write the number of the bus on each kid's right hand, that would be tremendous!"

"Sure thing!" Effie said, smiling and giving Cindy a wink.

"My name's Constance," the staff person said as introductions were quickly shared.

Cindy began writing bus numbers on the kids' hands, and it wasn't long before she was drawn into a conversation.

"What's up?" said one precocious boy, who looked about eight.

"Pardon me?" Cindy raised her eyebrows.

"You're new." He said, extending his hand. "My name's Wilson. And you don't need to tag me."

"Why not?"

"I know what bus I came on and I have a memory like a vault," he said, pointing to the side of his head.

"Pleased to meet you, Wilson."

He paused for a moment before moving the conversation forward. "And your name is?"

"Cindy."

"Well, Cindy, the first thing you need to know is that Brooklyn isn't Kansas."

"I didn't think it was." She couldn't help but smile. "And what makes you think I'm from Kansas?"

"You don't give off a big-city vibe," he said.

"No kidding."

"No offense, but it's the truth."

"Well, thank you for being so honest, Wilson."

"My mom says truth is more valuable than gold."

"From the mouth of babes," thought Cindy. "Isn't it a shame that these kids are robbed of their innocence before they even have a chance to experience it?" Suddenly, the reality of what she had just thought hit home.

"So, how do you like Saturday Sunday School?"

Wilson smiled. "It's cool. I mean, we get to play games, watch skits, and learn things." He paused just a moment to further size up Cindy. "And it beats hanging around home where no one cares if you're there or not."

His directness startled her. "I'm sorry."

He shrugged his shoulders. "My mom works nights. She says I'm old enough to take care of myself. So, I do."

Cindy didn't have time for a follow-up question because the line from Wilson's bus was ready to move inside the church building.

She barely had a minute to catch her breath when another crew of kids hopped off a bus, and Constance motioned for Cindy to help tag the kids.

One of them, a bright-eyed girl who couldn't have been more than six, pulled Cindy aside.

"As far as I'm concerned, all of this mumbo jumbo had better work!"

"Mumbo jumbo?"

"Yeah. My friend LaToya told me to come with her today. (LaToya had gone ahead to the building where the older kids went.) She said God hears you when you pray. Is that true?"

"Wow, talk about hitting the ground running!" thought Cindy. "And the ironic thing is, I feel exactly as this little girl does! In fact, I've been asking the very same question for years!"

"Well, it's going to be Christmas soon," Cindy said, deciding to take a neutral stance. "And it's a very special time of year."

"How's that?" the little girl asked. "Maybe you can talk to God for me. You might have better luck."

"I doubt that."

"Why not? You work here, don't you?"

"I'm just volunteering," she answered. "Anyway, we're all the same in God's eyes." She held out her hand before continuing. "I'm Cindy."

The little girl took hold of her hand like it was a lifeboat, squeezing with a surprising amount of strength. "Saree, with two e's." She nodded her head for emphasis. "I'm five and a half, but they let me come here because my mom died."

"I'm so sorry!"

"It was just after the Fourth of July when Mom died. There were a lot of fireworks going off in the street, so I was awake. I heard Grandma call the ambulance. Grandma told me that I have to be a big girl now. I asked LaToya about it because she's my best friend. She'd been telling me to talk to God about it, but I don't know how."

Cindy knelt down to be eye-level. "God, if you're out there, please give me something to say to this little girl! She needs you! I need you!" she prayed silently.

Slowly, the words came: "Saree, when I was 18 years old, I lost my younger sister. She and I were close. We were best friends, like you and LaToya. She was killed in a car accident."

"And everything changed, didn't it?"

"Yes."

"What did you do about it? Did you talk to God?"

"I talked to God a lot."

"Did it help?"

As the words were forming in Cindy's head, so was the revelation about their importance. "Sometimes when we talk to God, we forget to listen."

"LaToya says that's the most important part of being a friend."

Cindy nodded her head in agreement.

"Then that's your secret?"

"Saree, believe me. I don't have a special secret."

"I guess I'm too mad at God right now to listen very much."

"This little one is pulling at my heartstrings!" Cindy thought. "Of all the kids coming off all the buses, why did it have to be this one who strikes up a conversation?"

Instantly, the past twelve years of her life flashed past her. There were a series of accomplishments, to be sure, but one scene kept playing itself out again. It was a very angry older teen turning into a very sarcastic, unbelieving woman on the verge of becoming a bitter, middle-aged person.

There was no forgiveness, no mercy, no joy. Only judgment stemming from massive disappointment. The whole irony of the situation – that God would be present in this precious child who had lost her mother – wasn't lost on Cindy.

"Saree, when something really bad happens, you have a choice. You can either use that awful thing to let God get closer to you. Or you can use that awful thing as an excuse to blame God. Please take your friend's advice and listen to what God has to say to you."

Saree looked straight into Cindy's eyes. "Is that what you did?"

"I'm beginning to," she answered. For the first time in a long, long time Cindy allowed herself to smile openly.

"Thanks," said Saree, impulsively giving her a hug before heading into the building with the rest of her group.

"Hey there, stranger!" From across the parking lot, Effie strolled up. "How's it going?"

"You're right."

"About what?"

"This isn't like church at all."

The Emergency Room

Archie logged into the emergency room admitting desk's computer. It was Christmas Eve, and he had volunteered to take the second shift because he had no family to speak of, and he wasn't particularly the sort who celebrated holidays. Plus, he knew he'd be earning double-time and a half for doing it, so when he was asked to switch days, he was willing.

Connie, on the other hand, was slightly peeved. She was very social and attended St. Martin's Lutheran Church, which put on a magnificent midnight service, complete with carols sung by candlelight, a full-fledged choir, and a nativity scene. If she hadn't been an extremely dedicated ER aide, it might have made for a difficult evening. Since her shift would be over at 11, she'd still have plenty of time to meet her family at St. Martin's, but she would have to forgo the traditional Christmas Eve meal with them beforehand.

The hospital was a small one, and the ER had only six beds. Since space was at a premium, the triage area was three feet away from where Archie was working.

"Merry Christmas!" Connie said, popping her head into Archie's area in between checking on medical supplies.

Archie looked up from his PC and nodded.

"So, how many patients do you figure we'll see tonight?" she asked. It was standard practice for those working the ER second shift on a holiday to make a guess. The winner received a free dessert from the hospital cafeteria, courtesy of the rest of the department staff.

"The weather outside is good," Archie began. "I don't see us having a busy night. Maybe five."

"I'm going with a dozen," Connie said. She had a tendency to think in even terms. Growing up, she'd been a bit on the OCD side, and nurse aide training had only reinforced this. If there was one profession where it helped to be OCD, it was medical.

Archie was 25 and held a BA in English. He was working in a hospital due to owing something like $10,000 in student loans, which, comparatively speaking, wasn't a lot. In fact, he felt fortunate that he had gotten out of the hallowed halls of academia only owing what he did. His sister was good friends with the Director of Human Resources at the hospital, so that had given him an inside track. He got the job two years ago, right out of college, and had grown to like it. In fact, for a nonscientific-minded person, he found the hospital culture to be extremely interesting.

Although small, Lakeside General still needed personnel to run all the standard departments within it, including critical care, pediatrics, surgery, radiology, laboratory, respiratory therapy, and outpatient. And just like the outside world, individuals who worked in a hospital were a true cross section, and in general, they tended to form a more diverse group.

Maggie turned the corner from the small desk that served as the ER nurses' station and walked up to them.

"You know what they say about things," she said, with the self-confidence of a head nurse.

"What things?" said Archie.

"Things come in threes."

"Tell me you don't believe that," said Connie. "You're a nurse. You're supposed to be scientific."

To be sure, Maggie was levelheaded, but she was also a bit of an adventurer. In the summer of her fourth birthday, she received a red wagon as a present. She immediately took it up to the top of the street, a very steep climb, got in, and steered herself down the sidewalk that conveniently leveled out near her house. All the way down, she had a magnificent smile on her face.

The year before she got the red wagon, Maggie had almost given her mom a heart attack when she was told to stay in the car as her mom unloaded the groceries. True to form, Maggie got out, went to the front seat, put the car in reverse, and steered down the driveway.

Only a few seconds after Maggie had done this, her mom came out of the house and ran after the car, which thankfully came to rest safely across the street.

As her mom sprinted breathlessly up to the driver's window, Maggie announced, "I didn't take my hands off the steering wheel the whole time, Mom!"

Maggie had grown up to be a doer with hazel eyes, black hair, and an effortlessly sunny disposition.

While Maggie was the brains of the ER team that was working that Christmas Eve, Connie was the heart. She was short but a dynamo. Anyone who looked into her deep blue eyes instantly registered the compassion there. Anyone who worked with her for more than half a shift knew her energy level was always on high.

For the first two hours of the shift, from 3 until right before supper break, only one patient came through the ER doors. And that was a case of running out of a cholesterol-inhibiting prescription after hours.

Archie was the first to speak up: "I hate to say it, but I'd like to revise my initial estimate down."

"You can't. We're about to go on supper break, and you know the rules," Connie retorted good-naturedly.

"OK, then, can we discuss a book I'm reading?"

"Sure," Maggie answered. She was always game, being an avid reader herself.

"I'm reading *Bel Canto* by Ann Patchett. And I'm struck by something she wrote."

He pulled out the book from his backpack, turned to page 156, and began reading. The plot takes place in South America and concerns a rebel group that had taken over the house of the Vice President, holding about 30 people hostage while their demands were being considered.

> *Yes, the generals wanted something better for the people, but weren't they the people? Would it be the worst thing in the world if nothing happened at all? If they all stayed together in this generous house? Carmen (one of the rebel soldiers holding the hostages) prayed hard. She prayed while standing near the priest in hopes it would give her request extra credibility. And what she prayed for was nothing. She prayed that God would look on them and see the beauty of their existence and leave them alone.*

"I can see the story's got you hooked," Maggie said.

"I'm intrigued by Carmen's question. Why do religious-minded people always feel that it's a good idea for God to intervene? Why can't they be content with the beauty around us?"

Connie got up to stretch a bit. "I'll be the first to admit that life can be beautiful, but I would never ask for God to take his hands off us."

"Couldn't the human race get by with benign neglect? I mean, it seems like most of the problems we face happen when we try to fix things, either with or without God's help."

By now it was closing in on five o'clock, and Connie excused herself to get supper while the getting was good.

"I tend to agree with Nelson Mandela on that one," Maggie said.

"What do you mean?"

"There's a great quote of his that I love. 'There is no easy walk to freedom anywhere, and many of us will have to pass through the valley of the shadow of death again and again before we reach the mountaintop of our desires.'"

Archie nodded his head in agreement. "That's a good one. But what does it have to do with being content with the beauty around us?"

"Mandela's point was that we have to take responsibility. To be active."

"So, you're agreeing with me?"

"Not exactly. I see your starting point, but you and I are headed in different directions."

"How so?"

"Mandela probably prayed to God to change his situation. To change South Africa a lot."

"But he understood the power of a people's movement."

"He came to understand the power of forgiveness."

"He was the captain of his soul," Archie said emphatically.

"Either way, he didn't sit idly by."

"At the end of the day, he wasn't asking God to change South Africa. He was busy doing it himself."

Maggie came and sat down next to Archie. She understood the philosophical passion of being young. She was about 10 years older than him and not that far removed from Archie's experience. She had grown into her profession, starting off in the Intensive Care Unit and then proving herself capable of being head nurse. A few years after that, her thirst for new experiences caused her to apply for the ER position, where she quickly moved up to the head nurse position.

As the conversation kept going, Dr. Laughlin Packard came into the room after having taken care of the patient who needed his prescription refilled.

"How dumb is that?" he announced, interrupting the flow. "Waiting until Christmas Eve to realize you needed a medication refill? Guaranteed to leave you for at least two days without your meds. So, you not only take up our time, you get yourself billed for a $150 ER visit, which your insurance isn't going to pay."

"Life happens," said Maggie, shrugging her shoulders.

"That doesn't mean it has to be unnecessarily expensive."

Which was an ironic thing for Dr. Packard to be saying, given the fact that he had a reputation as being a bit of a spendthrift. In fact, he had chosen to take the Christmas Eve and Christmas Day shifts to earn extra money to help cover two weeks off in Aspen for his winter break.

"Doc, what do you think of today's subject?" Archie asked.

"I only caught the tail end. I love what Mandela said. He's a classic example of taking personal responsibility for your life. He strove for meaning in everything that he did."

"What about the God factor?" Maggie asked.

Dr. Packard shook his head. "In my world view, God isn't part of the equation. There's too much going on around us that points in the opposite direction of heaven."

"So, you think it's okay to pray to God to just leave us alone?"

The doctor laughed before responding. "That's a good one, Archie! As far as I'm concerned, if I even believed in God, I'd say God's already doing a great job of that."

"If you argue from the point of creation, even if you aren't a creationist, you are left with facing the fact that existence didn't just happen. Matter has to come from somewhere. It has to have a force behind it," Maggie said.

Just then, the second patient of the Christmas Eve evening came through the door. A family. Mom, Dad, and a three-year-old.

Archie sprang into action.

"May I help you?" He asked the question to the group in general.

"It's my daughter," the dad said, looking frightened. "There was a fire in the apartment next to ours."

"The fire station's right down the street, and they put out the fire before it had a chance to spread much," the mother continued. "But there was smoke damage, and my daughter has asthma."

Archie stayed with the dad and quickly finished up the beginning of a chart on his computer, hitting the submit button.

Meanwhile, Maggie motioned for the mom, who was holding their daughter, to come to the closest exam bed.

Dr. Packard took over from there, glancing over the chart that now appeared on his own PC.

"So, there was a fire in the apartment next to yours?"

"Yes, and it triggered an asthma attack."

"Is your daughter being treated?"

"She's on a bronchodilator."

Dr. Packard did a routine exam, including the lungs and heart, and nodded to the mom.

"The smoke was noxious enough to trigger a reaction that needs something to boost what you're currently using and get her lungs back to normal."

After administering the shot, the young girl began to breathe normally within a minute.

At this point, the dad came into the exam room, visibly relieved to see his daughter breathing with no strain.

"She's going to be fine," Dr. Packard said. "My only concern is that you have an alternative place to stay for a few days while the smoke damage is cleared out of the apartment next to yours."

The mom nodded her head. "On the way here, I called my cousin. We can stay with her temporarily."

"Good. Then keep using the bronchodilator, as prescribed."

And that was that, after which Dr. Packard headed to the cafeteria as Connie rejoined the group.

"What'd I miss?" she asked.

Maggie gave the update: "A little girl's asthma was triggered by an apartment fire next door. She was treated and released just a few minutes ago. Which sort of proves my point."

"What point?" Connie asked.

"That we need God's intervention to get us through the day."

"Did you catch the address on the patient's chart?" Archie asked.

It was a street nicknamed "Project Hill." Half of the apartments were in large, barrack-style row houses, built at the outset of World War II to house military families. They were set up quickly as a short-term fix and never intended for anything else, let alone decades-long inhabitance. They were, by far, the cheapest housing available in the city, and landlords skirted the housing code violations by simply selling the buildings to someone else.

Kids growing up in these apartments went to a school about half a mile away. And educators there knew that, on average, a third of their students who started in September would leave before the end of the year, their families being chased by the same landlords.

He kept on. "Tell me how God is watching out for these kids. How in the world does anyone learn to rely on anyone or anything growing up in such an unstable neighborhood?"

Connie looked Archie in the eye, "God hasn't abandoned those kids."

As much as she wanted to stay and be part of the conversation, Maggie knew it was time to head for supper, leaving Archie and Connie to hold down the fort temporarily.

"How can you possibly say that?" Archie asked.

His own parents had been superlative in their child-rearing, raising three children – Archie and two older sisters. Being the youngest, Archie had the advantage of seeing love in action until cancer took his father when the young boy was a senior in high school. The cancer had been especially aggressive. Within six months of being diagnosed, Archie's father was gone. The family hadn't been churchgoing, so the blow was felt without the comfort of a belief system. For Archie, his father's passing had become the defining moment of his life.

"God knows about those families," she began. "Their suffering isn't happening in a vacuum. To us, looking in from the outside, it may seem like it. But that's not the case. A person's soul is the most resilient creation on the planet."

"But that little girl who was treated tonight. She's growing up in horrible living conditions."

"But her parents care for her. They brought her in to get treatment."

"Directly related to the housing project they're living in because they can't afford anything better for their family. Where's God in that?"

"You and I don't know the whole story. We see the shell, but God sees the entire situation."

At this point, the conversation was put on hold when a call came in from a 911 dispatcher, letting them know an ambulance was on the way.

Within a few minutes of Connie paging Dr. Packard, the ambulance pulled up.

"The patient fell on her left side at home; her vital signs are stable, but the patient's complaining of pain and her inability to move on the affected side," one of the ambulance attendants stated as the patient was wheeled into the examination area.

Almost as soon as Archie had begun a chart, an elderly gentleman walked through the ER doors.

"I'm with the ambulance," he explained. "My wife, she was repositioning the Christmas star on our tree, and she overreached and fell to the side, and I couldn't get her up."

"Onto her left side?"

"Yes."

"Does she have any medical conditions or allergies?"

"She's taking medication for high blood pressure. That's all. And she doesn't have any allergies that we know of."

Archie entered this additional information into the computer so Dr. Packard, who was now back in the ER and doing a preliminary exam on the man's wife, would have it.

Despite the circumstances, the gentleman remained calm.

"The name's Grayson," he said, sticking out his hand towards Archie. "Grayson Alexander. Olivia's my wife."

The times that handshakes were exchanged in the ER were few and far between; nonetheless, Archie extended his own hand towards Grayson. "Archie," he said, "Archie Mason."

"Thank you for taking care of my wife."

Archie smiled. "Well, I'm actually not the one doing anything medical. Just gathering information."

"You're part of a team, and I thank you."

Maggie came back from supper, turned the corner to Archie's desk, and nodded towards the cafeteria, indicating it was his turn to go.

"Mr. Alexander, it's a pleasure to meet you," he said. "I'm headed for supper now, but your wife is in good hands."

Maggie was briefed on Mrs. Alexander's condition and the fact that she'd been sent to have an x-ray. Meanwhile, she and Connie joined Mr. Alexander in the waiting room.

"Your wife was just sent to radiology," said Maggie.

"We want to be sure that she hasn't broken any bones," explained Connie, heading back into the ER to cover for Archie.

"I'm just thankful it wasn't anything worse," he said, adding, "We've been married 50 years."

"That's a long time!"

"Yes, the good Lord has been kind. Can you believe we've never had a major accident until tonight? Christmas Eve of all days!"

"Well, things happen, Mr. Alexander. Holidays are usually busy for us."

"I guess that makes sense. People are coming and going, and they're in a hurry."

Maggie decided to change the subject. "So, were you born and raised here?"

"Oh, no," he smiled. "My family's from Alabama. We didn't move up until 1947 when my dad got a job at Ford."

"Those were good-paying jobs."

"Previous to that move, Dad was a sharecropper."

"Where was that?"

Mr. Alexander looked up at Maggie. His eyes were as bright and clear as his mind. He could have told her the usual stuff: the number of times he'd been back to see the old homestead. Or share a funny story or two about his extended family. But he saw something in Maggie that told him she wouldn't be satisfied with anything superficial.

"Our family lived about 20 miles from Selma," he began. "We lived in the country, but every time we had business in the city, we'd have to encounter prejudice. Some of it was blatant, some of it not so."

"I'm sorry," Maggie responded.

He shrugged his shoulders. "That's just the way it was. Until 1965. Because we still had family ties there, we knew what was happening in Selma. I was a young man in college by then, and I just couldn't abide standing by. So, when I heard about Dr. King's plan to march from Selma to Montgomery, I knew I had to be there."

"So, you were a Freedom Rider then?"

"No. I wasn't that organized about it," he laughed. "I drove down from Michigan with a friend, and we stayed at my cousin's place. The three of us joined the march with all the others who wanted to change the world."

"And you *did* change it."

"Well, I don't know about the world, but that experience certainly changed me."

Maggie was curious. "How so?"

"The person who shared a ride to Selma became my wife." He laughed after he offered that tidbit.

"Wow!"

"We really didn't know each other that well before the trip. We had taken some classes together at the University of Detroit. So at least we had something in common."

"Sounds like you two really hit it off."

"Not at first. But gradually, as we shared about our families and our histories and what drew us to Selma, we became friends. And by the end of the semester back at school, I proposed to Olivia."

"That's quite a story," Maggie said, impressed. Not just with Mr. Alexander's story, but with the way he conducted himself, with a quiet dignity seldom seen in a crisis.

"Well, my wife and I, we've always agreed on two things."

"What's that?"

"We try to do something every day to make a difference in someone's life. Even if it's just treating a neighbor with kindness. And we are determined to live out our faith. For us, the two go hand in hand."

Just at that moment, Olivia Alexander was wheeled back to the ER.

Dr. Packard came back shortly after conferring with the radiologist on call.

"Mrs. Alexander, I'm happy to report that there's no fracture or break in your pelvic area," he said. "I'd say you were given holiday amnesty."

Mr. Alexander had joined them in the examination room. "I'd say it was grace from God," he said.

"Either way, sir, your wife appears to have been spared any complications. We'll give her a prescription for pain to help with the soreness she'll likely feel over the next week or so."

"Thank you, Doctor," Olivia spoke up. "I appreciate your service. Especially tonight."

"You're welcome," Dr. Packard smiled. "Happy Holidays!"

Olivia looked directly at Dr. Packard. "Merry Christmas!"

"I'm afraid I don't celebrate that holiday," he said matter-of-factly.

Archie walked back into his office area just as Maggie handed Mrs. Alexander her prescription along with two days' worth of the same medication.

"This should get you through Christmas," she said.

As Connie wheeled Mrs. Alexander towards the front door, Mr. Alexander went up to Archie's desk.

"Son, don't sell yourself short."

"Pardon?" The statement caught Archie completely by surprise.

"Your life isn't accidental."

Mr. Alexander had no way of knowing the conversation that had already taken place, which included Mandela, and

Carmen's prayer for benign neglect. But Maggie had told Archie the short version of how the Alexanders had gotten to know each other on the way to Selma.

"Sometimes it seems like it," Archie responded.

"We aren't called to live our lives based on feelings. If I had, I would never have gotten to know Olivia and we wouldn't have married and spent 50 years together."

"But the days of Freedom Riders are long gone," Archie sighed, wishing he had a cause to believe in.

Mr. Alexander shook his head. "Son, I believe that each generation has a cause. It's placed deep inside your heart. Nelson Mandela's cause was forgiveness. And when he learned how to express it, that forgiveness forged a path to an entire country's freedom." He paused a moment before continuing. "And it began with one person. Remember what Mandela said?"

Archie felt something like a bolt of electricity shoot through him as he repeated the quote that Maggie had mentioned earlier in the evening. "'There is no easy walk to freedom anywhere.'"

Mr. Alexander's smile lit up the ER lobby as he turned to drive his wife home.

The Redemption of Campbell

Campbell had a memory ten times that of your average elephant, so of course, she remembered what time she had told Everett to meet her in the lobby of Miller Auditorium. And she was well aware that he was already fifteen minutes late.

"I just don't get you!" she said when he finally showed up.

"Get what?"

"Get how you show up by suddenly appearing, as if there's no such thing as time."

"I was a little late!" he replied.

"With no viable excuse!"

Everett shrugged. "Who needs an excuse for being a little late?"

"You do!" she said, keeping her tone soft. "Because for you, being late is the norm, and it's rude."

At this point, Everett simply looked straight into her brown eyes and smiled sarcastically. "So is castigating your date in public."

He turned and walked out, right past the row of Christmas trees that adorned the lobby.

Under normal circumstances, Campbell would have had something very much like a panic attack. But instead of calling his name out, or running after him, she slowly walked away from the Will Call window and slumped down on a bench.

"Why do they call it Will Call, anyway?" she thought. "Whoever came up with that term sure had the glass-is-half-full outlook down pat."

Then Campbell felt a slight tap on her left shoulder. Looking up, she saw Duncan with a smile on his face.

"I'm so sorry," he began. "Are you okay?"

"I didn't leave a trail of blood, did I?"

Duncan smiled and shook his head. "No, but word on the street is that you need to enforce the two-feet rule with a guy like that."

"Pardon?"

"You know, personal space and safety issues and all that. Sometimes what you say sounds different from two feet out."

Campbell heaved a sigh. "But he was right. What I did embarrassed him. And no one gets anywhere by embarrassing a friend."

"I was going to ask you if you do that sort of thing often, but that would only be reinforcing your point, right?"

She smiled weakly and nodded her head.

"So, what's your next move?" he asked.

"I'd be doing great to get up from this bench and walk out of the lobby as unobtrusively as possible. I'm assuming you caught my Oscar-winning putdown." Campbell started to cry.

Duncan offered a Kleenex. "I manage the box office, so I couldn't help but overhear."

She blew her nose and slowly got to her feet. "What is it with men, anyway?"

"I don't know," he answered half-heartedly. "I'm one of them."

Duncan was 44 years old. He wasn't a spring chicken by any means, but good DNA made up for it. Black, wavy hair, very approachable, in a Paul Rudd-ish sort of way, especially if you saw *Ant-Man* or *Admission*.

Campbell was in the same age group, give or take a year or two, and had deep brown eyes that were almost black.

"It's hard, always seeming to attract the wrong sort of person," she said.

Duncan put both his hands in the air in mock surrender, then shrugged his shoulders.

"I have to get back to work," he said. "And speaking on behalf of the entire Western Michigan University box office staff, let me say that we hope that your next experience with us is a peaceful one."

She smiled despite herself and walked out.

In every other aspect of her life, Campbell was satisfied, if not downright happy. She lived in Kalamazoo and loved it. After ten years working as an assistant marketing director, she had gone on to establish her own consulting firm and enjoyed the challenge. She lived in an upscale condo development off Drake Road. She had great neighbors and two cats. Her parents and three siblings all lived in Michigan and regularly got together. Life was good, except for a major hole in the relationship department.

Soon after the incident at Miller Auditorium, Campbell was sitting on her condo patio, admiring the view into the woods nearby, when her phone rang. She picked it up on the third ring, not recognizing the number.

"Hello?" she began.

"Could I please speak with Campbell?" came the voice on the other end.

"Speaking."

"It's Duncan from the Miller Theatre Box Office. The guy who gave you a Kleenex a few nights ago?"

A tidal wave of shame rushed over her.

"How in the world did you get my number?"

"Well, we've got your contact information on file here, and one of my ticket takers matched your seat number to the performance that you didn't wind up attending."

"So, tell me," she asked, "do you always do follow-up psychological assessments on disgruntled performance-goers?"

Duncan laughed out loud. "I wanted to see if you'd like to grab a cup of coffee sometime."

It wasn't as if Campbell was eager to spend time with a witness to her social gaffe, but, on the other hand, her experience with Duncan led her to believe that he was genuinely kind, and at least thoughtful enough to lend a hand under trying circumstances.

"If I say yes, what am I setting myself up for?" she thought. "I don't want another in a series of misguided relationships. Maybe this is God's way of saying I'm better off being a hermit. But if that's true, then why haven't I moved to South Dakota? Not to mention, shouldn't I be working on my friendship skills instead of having coffee? On the other hand, Duncan seems decent enough. It's only coffee, for heaven's sake!"

"Sure. Coffee sounds great. And I promise not to be wearing a watch."

They decided to meet at Panera's on West Main Street that Saturday morning.

After turning off her cell phone, Campbell slumped down on a patio chair and looked up at a batch of cumulus clouds floating by. Her mind started to drift until she noticed that one of the clouds looked a lot like the profile of Regan, one of her former boyfriends.

They had met in senior seminar at Hunter College in New York City. They were both in the Creative Writing curriculum and began their relationship by reviewing each other's work. One week before graduation, they were sitting in a restaurant on Lexington and 76th Street. Campbell knew she was headed back home to Michigan soon, while Regan was poised to tackle life in the big city.

He had the good fortune of being an excellent networker, and it didn't hurt that his faculty advisor had connections with *The New York Times*. Through that connection, he had gotten a job interview in the research department. It wasn't frontline journalism, but it was a way to gain credentials and a foot in the door.

Campbell had no prospects at the moment but was looking forward to getting back home. Her degree was flexible enough that she wasn't worried about earning a living just yet.

Over coffee, Regan told her about his good fortune with *The Times*. He spoke of the possibilities and excitement of working for a world-class news organization. How his writing portfolio impressed his new boss. He told her that he had found two roommates to make living in the city a possibility: a walk-up on 14th Street, a quick subway ride uptown to work, within walking distance of The Village and his favorite Italian restaurant. He paused to take a sip of coffee in the middle of an already fifteen-minute review of his life, asking no questions about Campbell. When he finally got around to asking her how she was doing, he quickly looked at his watch and said he had to go.

"How could I ever have wasted any time with that guy?" she had asked herself while opening the coffee shop door and getting absorbed in the shuffle of Lexington Avenue. "What in the world is wrong with me?"

Why Campbell would consider that something was wrong on her end was because it wasn't the first instance of a one-way relationship. She had noted her inability to speak up for herself when it came to conversations while dating. Take, for instance, Treavor. They had met two years after

Campbell had landed a job as the Events Coordinator at the Barnes & Noble in the Southland Mall.

He participated in one of those local author gatherings. He came to the event with a friend's Labrador because someone had recommended that a canine companion at such things was a guaranteed crowd-pleasing magnet. Unfortunately, the day of the group book signing was also the first day of winter weather in Kalamazoo, and only a handful of people braved the snow to show up.

Feeling somewhat responsible for the lack of an audience and sales, when Treavor smiled and asked if she'd like to grab a cup of coffee after the event was over in the store's Starbucks, she felt compelled to agree.

For a half hour, Treavor talked about his social media presence and the number of people who had put his book "on the shelf" on Goodreads, while bringing up, in detail, how women had a challenge separating the "real" Treavor from his writing. It was all Campbell could do to stay awake, despite enough caffeine to keep a horse on the racetrack long after the race was over.

"So, what do you think?" Treavor had said, smiling.

"About you?" she had said.

"Of course!" he said, completely oblivious.

"Well, I think that the horrible weather we had tonight in no way limited sales for your book." With that, she got up and went home.

This was the epitome of being passive-aggressive, at least in the sense of not knowing how to appropriately express anger, but knowing that didn't help Campbell cut it out of her life.

She tried therapy and although it didn't give her much additional insight into her behavior, it did give her the confidence to get another job. Hence the move to marketing, which she loved. She also had an attraction to Watson, the head copywriter who handled most of the media relations work for the firm's major clients.

Watson and Campbell dated off and on for a year and a half.

It was over a dinner at Bangkok Flavor that things began to get interesting when Watson started talking about his life and how he wanted her to play a supporting role in it.

"We should really take this to the next level," Watson had said, raising his eyebrows for emphasis.

"What level?" Campbell had asked innocently enough.

"You know, this," he said, pointing to the two of them for emphasis.

"This," she put down her fork and looked at him directly, "is called eating. And I would assume that the next step is digestion."

"What's that?" he had asked, innocently enough.

"Good heavens, you haven't even heard me!" Campbell said. "I think the only person you want to take it to the next level with is yourself."

She put her napkin on the table, took out twenty dollars to cover her meal, plunked it down, and left.

That had happened a year ago, and the only other person she had dated since then had been Everett, who had come late to the Will Call window.

Which leads us back to Duncan.

He was a native of Bloomfield Hills who made the trek to the western part of the Great Lakes state to attend college. He graduated from Hope College, majoring in literature. He took a job as a substitute teacher for a few years before getting the job in the Miller Auditorium box office, working his way up to manager.

Duncan was one of those rare people who had a heart of gold. He genuinely enjoyed being around people and helping them. His eyes were brown, and they were outstandingly kind.

Growing up, he had been best friends with his next-door neighbor, who happened to be a girl. They went to the same school together through high school. Senior year, a week from the prom, Duncan and Trish were sitting in a pizza place. He was gathering up the courage to ask her to be his date when Trish picked up the conversation.

"I have such good news!" she had said.

He smiled, encouraging her to continue.

"I'm going to the prom with Jeff Danielowitz. He asked me this afternoon."

Duncan was crestfallen, but he didn't show it.

"Jeff's a great guy," he had said.

"So, who are you going with?" Trish asked.

"The possibilities are endless, so it's really hard to choose," he had lied.

He was polite to a fault, unpretentious, giving, and genuinely interested in others.

When he sat across from Campbell at Panera's, he was totally open to a new experience. He had made the phone call to her out of curiosity and a sense that here was a hurting human being who could use a friend.

When Campbell walked through the front door of Panera's, she immediately saw Duncan standing off to the side. His smile was genuinely contagious. They quickly ordered and sat down.

"Thank you for meeting me," Duncan said.

"Sure," Campbell said. "I usually don't respond to invitations from people that I don't know, but I felt it was time to take a chance."

"Change can be a good thing."

"That's for sure!"

"So, other than attending concerts on a regular basis, what other interests do you have?"

Campbell blushed. "You know the frequency of my concert going?"

Duncan held up his hands. "Well, only the ones through our venues at WMU. From the looks of things, you really like live theatre."

"I do. I mean, it's a safe place to get emotional, isn't it?"

"The whole element of catharsis?"

"Yes. But it's more than that. For me, theatre is a lifesaver if there ever was one."

"No kidding!" he said, leaning forward. "I've heard theatre described in a lot of ways, but that's unique."

"Why in the world did I just say that?" Campbell thought. "I've made it a point to deliberately stay away from talking about my past, and here I just opened the door wide open."

She sat there for a moment before continuing. "It's just easier to get angry in a crowd."

Duncan raised his eyebrows. "Why is that?"

"Growing up, I was taught that anger was bad and that I wasn't being good if I expressed that particular emotion. So, going to public performances, especially plays, allowed me to freely express that emotion."

"You must have loved Les Misérables!"

"That's one of my favorites!" she said. "I identified with Javert! He was so shortsightedly mean."

Duncan began to quote from Javert's suicide, spoken right after he was spared from death by Jean Valjean. Javert had been pursuing him because Valjean had escaped from prison, sent there for stealing a loaf of bread.

Vengeance was his
And he gave me back my life!
Damned if I'll live in the debt of a thief.
Damned if I'll yield at the end of the chase.
I am the Law and the Law is never mocked.
I'll spit his pity right back in his face!"
There is nothing on this earth that we share
It is either Valjean or Javert!

Duncan continued. "He was unable to accept forgiveness."

"Forgiveness outside of the law was incomprehensible to him."

"But mercy triumphs over justice, doesn't it?"

Campbell looked puzzled. "What?"

"It's from the Bible. In God's eyes, mercy is more important."

Now it was Campbell's turn to lean in. "Would you like to know why I love Javert's character?"

"I'm all ears."

"Because he reminds me of my own rigid, judgmental nature."

"Okay."

"And that makes me so angry!" Campbell began to cry.

For the first time in a long time, she allowed herself to feel deep frustration. Duncan pulled out a handkerchief, handing it to her.

"You don't go anywhere without them, do you?" she said, in between blowing her nose.

"It comes with being part of the entertainment industry. And booking our share of dramas at Miller."

She smiled. "I keep on repeating the same mistakes, and I'm getting too old for this sort of nonsense. Not to mention it's going to be Christmas soon, the season of peace and joy, which only accentuates the pain of those of us who don't have it."

"But there's a way out," he offered.

"Therapy? I've tried that. It didn't work."

Duncan shook his head. "That guy in the Will Call line. You said afterwards that it was your fault. It was almost as if you couldn't help getting angry with him."

"That's right."

"But I don't think you were angry with him at all."

"Pardon?"

"You said it just a minute or two ago. You're frustrated with your own self." Duncan paused. "Do you want me to continue? I mean, it's only an observation, for what it's worth."

"Go for it. I don't want to wake up on Christmas morning with a lump of coal in my stocking."

"What I think you need to ask is what are you afraid of?"

Campbell sat bolt upright. "I may be a lot of things, but I'm not afraid."

Duncan slowly raised his eyebrows. "You don't have to be conscious of something to be afraid."

"So, you think I'm allowing fear to rule over me? So, it causes me to treat guys badly?"

"From what I saw a few days ago, I'd have to say it's pretty much an automatic reaction, and from outward appearances, it seems to be based on fear."

"How can you say that? You don't know me well enough. Apart from having an extraordinary sense of when someone's going to be late."

Duncan nodded. "But I don't have to know a person to sense fear coming out of them."

Duncan hadn't always been so perceptive. Case in point: right after Trish told him who she was going to the prom with, he had tried with all his might to appear outwardly calm.

The problem was that on the inside, he was crushed.

Why is it that the nicest guys never seem to make it to the dance floor? Instead of channeling his energy elsewhere, he could have admitted disappointment. He could have looked Trish squarely in the eyes and said, "Look, Trish, I know it's probably too late, and this doesn't make a lot of sense, but we've known each other since we started walking, and I have to say this, or else I'll regret it forever."

He could have gone on to tell her how he truly felt and placed his chips on the side of honesty. But this wasn't a movie where that sort of thing readily happens. This was real life. And besides, Duncan had no emotional energy left. So, he let it slide. And in so doing he got into the habit of being the 'nice guy' who always deferred to others.

Campbell was sipping her latte when suddenly a smile began to appear. It was totally against her normal defense mechanisms.

"Are we having fun yet?" he asked.

"I'm thinking about what you said, and it makes sense. I've been to four different therapists, and they probably said the same thing you just did, but I wasn't ready to listen to them."

Duncan shrugged his shoulders. "Sometimes timing is everything. We've got to be in the right frame of mind to receive."

From out of nowhere, Campbell felt a wellspring of genuine appreciation. "Thank you," she said.

"For what?"

"For opening my eyes and helping me start to make emotional sense of things."

"Well, I'd love to sit here and take the credit for that, but you're the one who is processing any healing right now."

"Thank you," Campbell said again, smiling, "for the Christmas present!"

Winnie's Socks

Winnie was hoping against hope that people wouldn't notice that her socks didn't match. She had gotten up that morning way too excited to care what she put on her feet. As long as they were warm, what did it matter?

She herself didn't notice that they were two very distinct colors until she was going through the lunch line at Kalamazoo's Linden Grove School where she was in the eighth grade.

Her favorite subjects were reading, writing, and history. Especially African-American history, most of which she was learning on her own, outside of the classroom.

"Did you know that Zorah Neale Hurston wrote *Their Eyes Were Watching God* when she was in Haiti?" she asked Tashana. They were best friends because they both read at the 10th grade level, and their intelligence wasn't far behind that marker.

"What was she doing there?"

"Well, you know she was a great writer, but she was also an anthropologist."

"Right. But I didn't know the timing of things in her life."

Winnie nodded as Tashana continued. "Don't look now, but your socks are mismatched, big time."

"What?" She started to glance down.

"I told you not to do that! One of them is green, and the other is red."

"That's a relief," Winnie said, genuinely happy.

"Why is that in any way good news?"

"Because it's our last day of class before Christmas break, and I can say I chose Christmas colors to celebrate the occasion!"

Winnie was thoughtful as well as smart and indefatigably upbeat.

"You would say something like that."

"Why not? Maybe my subconscious was trying to send me a message to lighten up for the holidays, and I'm just now catching up. Speaking of which, what are your plans?"

Tashana set down her tray next to Winnie and let out a heavy sigh. She was prone to being the more dramatic of the two. "Let's just say that we tend to get into a sarcastic mode come the end of October, and we don't snap out of it until mid-January."

"That's sad."

"It's survival. How else are we supposed to deal with all the holiday syrup? It's enough to drive a person to stop eating sugar altogether."

Which, in Tashana's case, wouldn't have been hard to do. The only candy bar she ate was PayDay, and that was because she had something of a culinary fixation on peanuts. As far as other forms of candy, she didn't have a massive desire in that direction. As for cookies, peanut butter cookies were her favorite.

"But don't you like Christmas?" Winnie innocently asked.

It was Winnie's favorite time of year. In the first place, she loved wintertime, especially in Michigan, where there was snow. She loved walking in it. She loved skating – not the kind in ice arenas, but outside, on frozen ponds. She enjoyed trips to the Portage Ice Rink as well. The fact that Christmas happened to fall in the middle of winter only enhanced its attraction.

"No, I don't especially," Tashana said, frowning. "You know how my family feels about organized religion. They aren't big fans."

That was putting it mildly. Tashana's mom taught philosophy. Her dad was an engineer. They were both very tuned in to the practical world. It had rubbed off on Tashana and her older brother, Marcus, who was in dental school.

"But Christmas isn't about religion, Tashana."

If there were an eyebrow-raising Olympics event, Tashana would have won for her reaction to Winnie's statement. "Then please cue me in on what else is involved. Besides mass amounts of buying things other people don't really need?"

"Love came down," Winnie's answered.

"Oh, brother!"

You'd have to pardon Tashana on that one. She knew about existentialism before she had known anything about Jesus. It wasn't her fault that her parents were very social and often had friends over for dinner, and of course, the conversation around the table got a little deep at times. Tashana was used to asking for second helpings while the adults were discussing Nietzsche, Hegel, and Sartre.

"Give me a break, T. I know how you grew up." Whenever Winnie referred to her friend as "T," you knew she was getting serious.

"I'm not saying I understand it all. But it's hard to put the influence of my parents aside. It's in my DNA."

"There's more to life than our DNA."

"It predisposes us."

"It's nothing more than a collection of tendencies."

"That are hardwired. You can't deny it," Tashana argued.

"You can't deny that we have a spirit, too."

"This is the part where I tell you I'm about to lose interest."

Conveniently, just about then, Besse Mayfield sat down right across from them. Besse's hair was enormously curly and as close to fire-engine red as a human being could possibly get naturally.

"What's up, guys?" she said.

"We were talking about existentialism," said Tashana, really wanting to change the conversation.

"We were talking about Christmas!" said Winnie, really wanting to stay on track.

"I love it!" Besse shot back. "Christmas vacation is one of my all-time favorite subjects, next to recess and hall passes."

In case you may be wondering, Besse was the designated class comic. It wasn't that she had actually run for the position. As she herself explained it, "It's either make jokes or be really, really comatose."

"Besse, we were being serious!" said Winnie.

"So am I. The importance of rest and relaxation can't be over emphasized. Especially within the present-day public education milieu."

"What?" It was Tashana's turn to be annoyed.

"Perhaps you've heard the saying, 'All work and no play makes Ja'Quana a very dull egg.'"

"Life isn't a playground."

"Of course, it isn't. But it could be!"

Tashana and Winnie rolled their eyes, which gave Besse a few seconds to formulate a follow-up.

"Honestly, I was only trying to bring a little holiday cheer to the table," Besse countered. "Speaking of which, what are you doing Christmas Eve?"

"Nothing in particular," Tashana answered.

"Midnight mass!" said Winnie. "It's a candlelight service, and it's so beautiful. I love walking to St. Monica's. We don't live that far, and it's so peaceful that time of night. Especially if it's snowing. It's absolutely the best and—"

"Slow down, tiger." Besse put up her hand for emphasis. "I asked what you were doing, not how you felt about it."

"But the feelings make it special."

"Well, I'll be on a flight to Costa Rica!"

"Wow."

"Yeah, wow! My dad has been saving up for a big trip all year, and he's taking me there."

A day after her sixth birthday, Besse's father had come into the house and announced that he was leaving. It was the Fourth of July. The irony of the departure date wasn't lost on her.

"Dad, what's going on?" she had asked.

"Nothing in particular, sweetie," he had answered. At least he had the decency to let her know it wasn't her fault.

Winnie knew all about Besse's Independence Day experience. She not only knew about it; she could feel Besse's hurt every time she jokingly referred to it.

This would be a good time as any to let you know that Winnie's own upbringing was remarkably solid, especially when considering her two friends. She grew up with a dad and mom who enjoyed each other's company. In Winnie's family, mealtime meant everyone sitting around the table and free-fall engagement.

Simply put, it was a time to have a family-type conversation, with everyone having a chance to contribute and hear what each other had to say. As a little girl growing up, this was Winnie's first experience with listening and offering feedback in a non-judgmental, loving way. But as Winnie grew older, she realized that not everyone's life experience was the same.

To his credit, Bessie's dad had kept in touch with her even after moving out of state and across the country, mostly through yearly vacations and three weeks each summer spent with him.

"That's quite a Christmas present, going to Costa Rica," said Winnie.

"Yeah, it is." Bessie's face turned serious. "It just sucks a bit that we have to go out of the country to be together. I mean, I'm grateful for the experience, but I'd love to be with my dad more often."

"I'm sorry," was all Winnie could think to say, looking at the hurt in her friend's eyes.

"Parents are a mixed bag," said Tashana. "Nobody grows up free of complications. I'd trade you evenings discussing Nietzsche and Kierkegaard for Costa Rica any day."

"I try not to think about it too much. My motto is: It is what it is," said Bessie.

"But you're thinking about it now," said Winnie.

"It usually comes out at Christmas," Bessie explained. "I see all these other families hanging out together, and I get jealous. I wonder, do they even understand how fortunate they are to be normal?"

"Define normal, please," Tashana shot back. "If there is such a thing, I haven't bumped into it very often. And if we don't fit in, what are we then, freaks? Not to mention, we don't choose our families; we're born into them. Which puts us at a real disadvantage sometimes."

It got very quiet at their end of the cafeteria table as the strains of "The Christmas Song" came over the sound system. Mrs. Salapini, the proverbial 'Lunch Lady,' was a big one on setting ambiance in a very in-your-face way.

Chestnuts roasting on an open fire
Jack Frost nipping at your nose
Yuletide carols being sung by a choir
And folks dressed up like Eskimos...

"Good grief!" Tashana spoke first.

"That travesty of a song is exactly what I'm talking about!" said Bessie.

"Hey, it's classic Nat King Cole, Mel Tormé. Give them a break." Winnie felt compelled to defend them, and truth be told, she was a huge fan of Nat King Cole and loved the song.

"I can tell you, I was never a tiny tot with my eyes all aglow. I didn't believe in God. I sure as heck didn't believe in Santa Claus," Tashana replied.

"When's the last time you saw someone in your neighborhood roasting chestnuts on an open fire? If anyone tried that around here, they'd get arrested." Bessie was in high gear now.

"It's mostly a big-city thing now," said Winnie. "And anyway, that's not the point."

"Which is?" Bessie and Tashana said in unison.

"Chestnuts, mistletoe, turkey, walking in the snow—it's all part of it."

"Part of what?" Again, they spoke as one.

"Part of a bigger picture, guys. Christmas is the one time of year that we slow down and notice each other. It's about kindness and mercy and grace." Winnie was extremely patient.

"Where do you get this stuff?" said Bessie. "If you keep on believing that way, you are going to get seriously stepped on."

Winnie looked at Bessie and then Tashana. "I don't think that's what you honestly feel. There's no shame in being disappointed and remaining vulnerable."

There was a pause in the conversation. And another song came over the sound system. This time it was Judy Garland's rendition of "Have Yourself a Merry Little Christmas."

Have yourself a merry little Christmas,
Let your heart be light
From now on, our troubles will be out of sight

Have yourself a merry little Christmas,
Make the Yuletide gay,
From now on, our troubles will be miles away...

"See what I'm talking about?" offered Tashana. "Judy is asking for it. It's melancholy and morose. What is she trying to accomplish by shoveling all her hopes and dreams for friendship into one season of the year?"

"It's bad enough that it's not realistic, but it's spreading false expectations. Especially to people who can't afford to get hurt," Bessie offered. She didn't say that hers was a perfect example of a family that was split up to begin with and that would never have the luxury of gathering all together over the holidays.

"It's a wish, guys. Something to aim for, that's all," said Winnie, desperate to offer some semblance of peace. "There is always hope. And I believe that love wins."

"Says who?" asked Tashana to no one in particular.

"Would you like to hear the definition of love that I use?"

"Go for it," said Tashana, who despite herself, was finding that she was curious for the answer.

Love is patient and kind. Love is not jealous or boastful or proud or rude. It does not demand its own way. It is not irritable, and it keeps no record of being wronged. It does not rejoice about injustice but rejoices whenever the truth wins out. Love never gives up, never loses faith, is always hopeful and endures through every circumstance.

"Where did you get that?" Now Bessie's curiosity was piqued.

"It's from the Bible."

"Really," said Bessie, surprised. "I had no idea."

"It's poetic," said Tashana. "I wouldn't have guessed. Is that from some sort of updated version?"

Winnie laughed out loud. "No, not unless you count the New Living Translation as updated. It's mostly exactly how Paul wrote it a few thousand years ago."

"Paul who?"

"Paul of Tarsus. He wrote about half of the section of the Bible called the New Testament."

"Sounds like he was a major player," said Bessie.

"He didn't start out that way. At first, he was a major enemy. His specialty was tracking down people who had converted and having them killed. He thought they were heretics."

"What changed his mind?"

"He was on his way to shut down activity in Damascus. On the way there, he had what you might call a direct encounter with God."

"No kidding!" Bessie was all ears. "You mean like something extraterrestrial?"

"In a way. Paul was basically struck blind after God asked him why he was persecuting him."

"Struck blind? As in can't see anything? Or are you talking metaphorically?" Tashana wanted to be sure she understood the circumstances.

"I mean he was literally struck blind. It took a few days to recover his sight and during that time he had a major change of heart. He went from hating followers of Jesus to becoming one of them."

"Then what happened? Where did he get to the point of understanding love the way he did?" asked Tashana. "The man was obviously writing from personal experience."

"Yes, he was. But it took time," Winnie answered. "Paul wrote about being shipwrecked, run out of town, beaten, deserted, jailed, and put under house arrest for what he believed in. Not to mention that he was a leader in the established religious community before all this happened. He could have had a very comfortable life."

"So why the makeover? Where did the motivation come from?" asked Bessie.

"Love."

"As in 'love is patient, love is kind?'"

"Exactly," answered Winnie.

Tashana sat up straight. This conversation was taking her where her own life experience and philosophy hadn't ventured. "People don't normally choose to take on additional pain like he did."

"They don't," said Winnie, "unless they have a direct experience with love. He was as sane, as normal as you or me before being struck blind."

"And God was the one who struck Paul blind?" Tashana wanted verification, even as her mind was working overtime to process what had already been said.

"Yes. John, an original follower of Jesus, wrote that God is love. So, when you say that Paul was struck blind by God, it's equally true to say that he was blinded by love."

"But it sounds so absurd," said Bessie. "Taking away someone's eyesight doesn't seem like a loving thing to do."

"You have to remember it was only a temporary situation. And God provided Paul with a place to stay until he could see again. Plus, up until that Damascus experience, Paul was living from a motivation of rules and regulations. But he traded that in for a life based on relationship."

"He was emotionally blind," offered Tashana.

"Yes, that's a good way of putting it," said Winnie. "And that's why I get so excited about Christmas."

She had Bessie and Tashana's full attention.

"Because it's all about commemorating when love came to earth. We celebrate it. We can have our own Damascus experience and get our sight restored. We can be kinder and a little more gracious towards each other. To take our eyes off ourselves and onto others. Is that such a bad thing? Is that so hard to believe?"

"When you put it that way, no," said Bessie.

"I had no idea," said Tashana.

And as the three of them got up to leave the cafeteria, as if on cue, a final song came over the sound system, courtesy of Mrs. Salapini.

It came upon the midnight clear,
That glorious song of old,
From angels bending near the earth,
To touch their harps of gold:
"Peace on the earth, goodwill to men
From heavens all gracious King!"
The world in solemn stillness lay
To hear the angels sing...

Dan Salerno

ABOUT THE AUTHOR

A gentle man of faith, Dan Salerno (1952-2023) dedicated his life to social justice and helping those in need.

In addition to being active in his church (he was a Sunday School teacher for 25 years), he traveled on mission trips to Northern Ireland five times and to Japan.

He earned a Master's degree in Social Research from Hunter College and worked for the National Coalition for the Homeless while living in New York City. After 9/11, he worked for a children's ministry in Brooklyn for 16 months.

Dan held various positions at South Michigan Food Bank in Battle Creek during his 25-year tenure there. He retired in 2014 as Director of Fund Development.

Dan had extensive experience as a professional writer, supporting himself for several years as a freelancer. At various times he wrote for two south-central Michigan daily newspapers.

He also taught writing at a Michigan community college.

Ruby's Present and Other Warm Tales of Christmas is his third published book of short stories.